BRENDA
JACKSON

GUILTY PLEASURE

Love Passion & Promise

LOVE, PASSION AND PROMISE BOOKS are published by

The Madaris Publishing Company

P O Box 28267

Jacksonville, FL 32226

Cover design and layout by Nuance Art, LLC

Art direction by aCreativeNuance.com

ISBN :978-0-9799165-6-4

10 9 8 7 6 5 4 3 2 1

Printed in the United States of America

Love, Passion and Promise

An Imprint of the Madaris Publishing Company

www.madarispublishing.com

Dear Readers,

You have to love those "Bad News" Steeles.

When I introduced the Steeles with Chance Steele's story in *Solid Soul*, little did I know that I would be writing beyond Donovan's story, *Intimate Seduction*. But the more I wrote about the Steeles, the more I knew I had to tell you about their cousins - those other Steeles who live in Phoenix. They are the ones known as the "Bad News Steeles".

There are six brothers. So far you've been introduced to brothers Galen, Eli, Jonas and Tyson, and how they succumbed to love. Brothers Mercury and Gannon are still holding out, but we will see how long that last. Now in **Guilty Pleasure** you are reacquainted with Tyson's best friend, Cohen Carlson.

You met Cohen in Eli Steele's novel, A Steele for Christmas. You also met Eli's fiancé, Stacey Carlson's best friend Dee Lewis. Something has been going on between Cohen and Dee for a few years. Why are they keeping it secret? Why is Dee upset? Why is Cohen frustrated? You will get answers to all these questions when you read Guilty Pleasure.

And there are a few characters I suggest you put on the "To Watch" list. Heroes like Zion Blackstone, Justice

Lewis and Midas Coronado. Zion's book will be out in 2018. No dates yet on Justice and Midas' books, but they have been placed on my "To Do" list.

Thank you for making the Steeles a very special family. I love writing stories about their friends and look forward to bringing you more books of endless love and red-hot passion.

Happy Reading!

Brenda Jackson

ACKNOWLEDGEMENTS

To all my readers who asked for Cohen and Dee's story. This one is for you.

To Nuance Art. Thanks for such a beautiful book cover.

Though your beginning was small, yet your latter end would increase abundantly.

Job 8:7 KJV

**IN LOVING MEMORY OF THE MAN WHO WILL
ALWAYS AND FOREVER BE THE LOVE OF MY LIFE
GERALD JACKSON, SR.**

FEBRUARY 11, 1951 – DECEMBER 15, 2013

THE STEELE FAMILY AND FRIENDS NOVELS

The Charlotte, North Carolina Steeles

Solid Soul

Night Heat

Beyond Temptation

Risky Pleasure

Irresistible Forces

Intimate Seduction

The Phoenix, Arizona Steeles

Hidden Pleasures

A Steele for Christmas

Private Arrangements

Possessed by Passion

Bachelor In Demand Series

Bachelor Untamed

Bachelor Unleased

Bachelor Undone

Bachelor Unclaimed

Bachelor Unforgiving

GUILTY PLEASURE

BY
BRENDA JACKSON

PROLOGUE

Stacey Carlson paused at the entrance to the ballroom where Deidre Lewis's parents' fortieth wedding anniversary party was being held. She and Eli Steele had arrived in Memphis early that morning, so there was no reason for them to be arriving to the party late...other than the fact that Eli never placed a time limit on their lovemaking. She blushed while thinking about all they'd done, typical Eli Steele style.

"Is anything wrong, Stacey?"

She glanced up at Eli and smiled. "No, what could be wrong?"

He shrugged massive shoulders. "Are you trying to prepare for when you see Wallace and Gail together?"

Stacey would admit that she'd thought herself in love with Wallace Flowers, just like she'd thought Gail Taggart had been one of her closest friends. A week before their wedding, Wallace had called it off saying he was in love with Gail, not her. She'd never felt so heartbroken, humiliated and betrayed in her life. But all that was behind her now. In a few weeks, she would be marrying the handsome man standing by her side.

"I don't have to prepare for that. Trust me, Gail did me a favor. If she hadn't taken Wallace off my hands, I wouldn't be marrying you on Christmas day, now would I?"

Eli chuckled. "No, you wouldn't. But that doesn't mean I won't be tempted to knock the hell out of the guy when I see him, just from the humiliation he caused you by breaking your engagement the way he did."

She eased up close to Eli. "I'd go through it all over again if you could be my reward in the end. Forget about what Wallace did. Just remember that we got the better deal." She took his hand in hers. "Come on. I can't wait for you to meet Dee's parents and her two older brothers, Justice and Lawyer. And Cohen is supposed to be here tonight. I can't wait to see him again."

Cohen was the older brother Stacey adored. Recently he'd received a big promotion to Chief of Surgery at a Florida hospital. Not bad for a thirty-five-year-old. But Stacey knew it was most deserving. She was happy for him, although it had meant he'd had to relocate again. The first time, he'd moved from Tennessee to Phoenix. Now he was moving again.

"Justice and Lawyer? Is there a reason for those names?" Eli asked.

Stacey chuckled. "Yes. Like you, both of Dee's parents are attorneys, and their sons went into the profession as well. So when you meet them, you'll feel right at home.

With her hand firmly planted in Eli's, Stacey entered the ballroom and was instantly overwhelmed by all the bright lights and beautiful decorations. She immediately saw Deidre, who had been Stacey's best friend since high school. The last time they'd seen each other was a few weeks ago, when Deidre, whom everyone fondly called Dee, had come to Phoenix to assist in the planning of Cohen's going away party.

Stacey knew she and Dee had to talk at some point. She wasn't sure what had happened between Dee and Cohen the night of Cohen's going away party, but something *had.* Although Dee had never told her, Stacey was aware that Dee had loved Cohen since the time they were teens. Stacey had been certain her friend would outgrow her infatuation, but Dee never had.

When Dee saw them, she raced over to give Stacey and Eli a huge hug. "I was beginning to worry about you two," Dee said, smiling at them.

"Sorry, we sort of got delayed," Stacey said, grinning over at Eli.

Dee chuckled. "Yeah, I bet. Come on, my family has been waiting for you. They can't wait to meet Eli."

Stacey glanced around. "Has Cohen arrived yet?"

"Yes, he's here."

Stacey wondered if Eli had noticed the sudden bitterness in Dee's voice. She definitely had.

A few moments later, Eli had met Dee's family and Stacey could tell he liked them. She was glad because the Lewis's had always treated her like a second daughter, and they'd been there for her and Cohen when their parents and aunt had passed away.

Stacey kept glancing around for her brother. She didn't see him anywhere. Maybe he was outside on the terrace that overlooked Brighton Lake.

Dee had excused herself for a minute and Stacey and Eli were standing near the French doors, enjoying the evening breeze. What a wonderful night.

But her enjoyment was cut short when a couple approached them. While she'd known this meeting was inevitable, she'd still dreaded it. Because the couple was Wallace and Gail.

**

"Stacey, it's good seeing you again," the woman said, giving a smile that Eli Steele thought was as phony as a three-dollar bill.

He roamed his gaze over the woman, trying to figure out what in the hell she supposedly had over Stacey. He found nothing. Stacey was better looking in all aspects. And he couldn't help but notice the way Gail was staring over the rim of her wine glass at him. Female interest. He would recognize it anywhere. She was checking him out, right in front of her fiancé.

"Gail, Wallace. It's good to see you both," Stacey said. "I'd like you to meet Eli Steele, my fiancé."

It took everything within Eli to be a gentleman and offer his hand to them. "So, Gail, I understand you're the woman I should thank," he said, pulling Stacey close to his side.

"Thank?" Gail asked, a confused look on her face. "Why should you be thanking me?"

"For taking Wallace off Stacey's hands. Otherwise, I wouldn't be marrying her Christmas day."

"You're getting married this Christmas, Stacey?" a surprised Wallace asked.

"Yes," Stacey said, smiling brightly as she looked up at Eli. He smiled back indulgently.

"The two of you really seem to be happy about it," Wallace said in a mocking tone.

Eli chuckled. "You can't even imagine. Overjoyed is more like it." He then lifted Stacey's hand to his lips. Might as well play this up, while he had the chance.

Gail blinked upon seeing the ring on Stacey's hand and almost choked on her wine. "That ring. Is it by Zion?"

He'd deliberately lifted Stacey's hand to kiss it on purpose. Her ring was always an attention grabber and he knew it. "Yes. Zion is a good friend of mine."

"He is? Wow," Gail said. "That ring is gorgeous."

"Only the best," Eli interjected, "for the best. Stacey is everything I've ever wanted in a woman."

Gail leaned close to him and whispered, "Too bad Wallace didn't think so."

Eli felt Stacey flinch and that pushed him to say, "Then maybe I need to rephrase that. She's everything any *real* man would want in a woman."

Wallace stiffened his spine. "What are you implying?"

Eli met the man's glare. "I didn't imply. I said it. Just the way you did, by the choice you made. Personally, I'm satisfied that I got the best woman for me. I hope you can say the same. Now if you will excuse us."

And without another word, Eli went to lead Stacey away. But his woman wasn't going to let him have all the fun. Before he'd taken a step, Stacey added, "By the way Gail, I love your ring. I must admit that it looks better on your hand than it ever did on mine."

Then they walked away. Once they'd moved some distance away from the couple, Eli asked, "Do you mean to tell me that she's wearing your old engagement ring?"

"Yes. He added a couple of small diamonds to give it a new look, but it's the same. Dee had told me it was, but I didn't want to believe Wallace would be that cheap...or that Gail would let him. They deserve each other."

Eli stopped walking and pulled her into his arms. "I'm anxious to get back to our hotel room."

Stacey gazed up at him, her heart filled with love for the man who wanted to make her his. "I really want to see Cohen before we leave. Dee said he was here but I haven't seen him anywhere. Let's look out on the terrace."

Cohen was indeed out on the patio...but he wasn't alone. He and Dee were having a heated discussion; one Stacey felt that she and Eli had no business hearing. "I think we need to go back inside before they notice us," she whispered.

"I agree," Eli said.

GUILTY PLEASURE

They returned to the ballroom. "Let's mingle some more and wait until they finish." Stacey wasn't sure what Cohen had done to upset Dee, but her best friend was definitely giving him a piece of her mind.

**

Cohen Carlson gazed down at Deidre Lewis. She was a beautiful woman. Almost too beautiful, with her black shoulder-length straight hair, cocoa-colored face, high cheekbones, full lips and eyes as dark as a raven's wing. They were eyes that could snatch the breath from a man's body if he stared into them too long. But that was something he wouldn't do tonight. "Let it go, Dee."

"Can you look me in the face and tell me that sleeping with me meant absolutely nothing to you?"

He rubbed his hands down his face. No, he couldn't do that. He'd desired Dee ever since he'd noticed she wasn't a kid anymore. He, of all men, knew that there was no temptation like Dee Lewis in a pair of stilettos. And her long, gorgeous legs sealed the deal.

Cohen had debated the wisdom of coming to her parents' anniversary party. He figured she might still be upset about what he'd said to her a couple of weeks ago. However, they were words she'd needed to hear. There could never be anything between them. She deserved a man who would love her with everything he had...but he was not that man. Years ago, he'd fallen in love like that, and the breakup had nearly killed him. It was something he'd swore he'd never go through again.

"Cohen?"

"You want more from me than I can give you. A relationship between us won't work."

"Because of our ages."

It was more than an age thing for him. It was his way of protecting his heart. He'd never told anyone about Amanda Forrestal, how hard he'd fallen for her, Amanda's subsequent betrayal and the emotional breakdown he'd suffered as a result. He'd almost lost everything and he wasn't willing to risk going through it ever again.

"Like I said, Dee, let it go. There can never be anything between us." He glanced at his watch. Stacey and Eli should have arrived by now. As soon as he saw them, he would leave.

He still found it hard to believe that his younger sister was marrying Eli Steele, of the Phoenix Steeles. There were six brothers – Galen, Eli, Tyson, Jonas, Mercury and Gannon. For years, they had been known around Phoenix as the Bad News Steeles because of their womanizing ways. But not anymore. The oldest Steele, Galen, had taken a wife and Eli would be marrying Stacey in a few weeks.

"Fine, Cohen," Dee said, breaking into his thoughts. "You win."

He looked at her. "I win? I wasn't aware this was a contest."

She glared at him. "I will give you what you want. I won't throw myself at you again. I'll do my damnedest to forget you even exist. Goodbye. I hope you have a long and miserable life. You deserve it."

He watched as she turned on those gorgeous stilettoed heels and left him standing alone on the patio.

1

Two and a half years later

I appreciate you coming to Phoenix to help me with Eli's birthday party, Dee."

Dee smiled across the table at Stacey. The two were enjoying lunch at Easterling's, a favorite of hers whenever she visited Stacey. On special today was their mouth-watering chili. It didn't matter to Dee that this was a sunny day in May. As far as she was concerned, chili was the perfect food. She could eat it any day of the week or any month of the year. Obviously, the restaurant staff agreed.

"You call, I come. That's how things are between us. Besides, this is Memorial Day weekend. What better time to hang out with friends? And once I leave here, I'm headed to Virginia Beach for two weeks." Dee loved teaching but she was glad the school year was over. She intended to enjoy her summer.

"Why Virginia Beach? I remember when we'd look for any excuse to head to Daytona Beach."

When she didn't say anything, Stacey placed her glass of tea down on the table. "Let me guess. It has something to do with Cohen, who lives less than a two-hour drive away, in Jacksonville."

Dee wanted to look away but couldn't. "Why would Cohen have anything to do with it?"

"Hmm, you tell me."

Dee stared down into her tea. Although Stacey was her best friend, she'd never told her about what had transpired between her and Cohen. Mainly because Dee hadn't wanted to make Stacey choose between her best friend and her brother.

"Uhhh…I kind of made a fool of myself over Cohen, once or twice."

Stacey reached across the table and took her hand. "Trust me, Dee, we've all made fools of ourselves at one time or another."

Somehow, Dee doubted she and Stacey had ever been in the same situation. "Maybe. But mine were whoppers." She took a sip of her tea. "I guess it's time I leveled with you about the secret I've been keeping all these years."

"What secret? That you had a thing for Cohen? I already knew that. I've known for years."

"And you never said anything?"

"No. I figured you would tell me when you wanted me to know. But honestly, it wasn't hard to figure out. I think everybody knew. My aunt, your parents and even your brothers. Especially Justice."

Dee raised a brow. "Why especially Justice?"

"Because he's more observant, where you are concerned, than Lawyer is."

Dee knew that was true. There was an eight-year age difference between her and Justice, while there was only five between her and Lawyer. As the oldest, Justice had always looked out for her and Lawyer. Now that she thought about it, Stacey was probably right. She hid her face in her hands. "Oh my god. That's all I needed to hear."

"I'm convinced Cohen was clueless though, Dee. Being a doctor was his main focus."

Dee knew all about Cohen's devotion to his profession. No one could have been prouder of him when he'd gotten that chief of surgery position in Florida. But there was nothing between them now. She squared her shoulders. Since she was opening up to Stacey, she might as well get it all off her chest. "I seduced him. Twice."

She hadn't meant to blurt it out that way, but she couldn't take it back now. Evidently, her voice carried, because two women in a nearby booth looked over at her.

She wanted to crawl under the table. But Stacey, she noticed, was smiling.

Dee frowned. "What's so funny?"

"Cohen is such a workaholic. I didn't think my brother could be seduced."

Dee rolled her eyes. She lowered her voice, so she didn't send the women still staring at her into cardiac arrest, and said, "Any man can be seduced, Stacey. Even a workaholic like Cohen. Trust me, I studied hard and planned well."

Stacey lifted a brow. "Studied hard and planned well?"

"Yes, I had no intention of failing. I bought every book I could afford on the art of seduction."

"You're kidding, right?"

Dee shook her head. "No. Once I'd figured out how to pull it off, I went to his apartment. He'd been out of town, but I knew he would return that night. And when he did, I was there, waiting for him."

Stacey's eyes widened liked saucers. Now it was Dee's turn to be amused. "What's wrong? You didn't think I had it in me?"

"Honestly, no. When was this? How did you get into his apartment?"

"It was when we were both right out of college, when you and I shared that apartment in Memphis. I borrowed your key."

Stacey lifted a brow. "My key?"

"Yes, the spare one he'd given you. You kept it on that key-rack that hung in the kitchen."

"You used that key to get into Cohen's apartment?" Stacey asked, shocked.

"Guilty as charged. I overheard your phone conversation with him earlier that day. He told you he was on his way back to Memphis from a medical convention in Dallas. So I put my plan into action, while I had the nerve to do so."

Dee saw that Stacey, who took another shaky sip of her iced tea, was hanging on to her every word, so she continued. "When he got home, I was there waiting for him." There was no need to tell Stacey that she'd also been in his bed, naked.

Stacey swallowed. "And he didn't ask you to leave?"

"Yes. In fact, I thought he was going to toss me out. We were arguing and then the next thing I knew, we were kissing. Things happened pretty quickly after that."

When Stacey didn't comment, Dee added, "He wanted me as much as I wanted him. I took advantage of that. It was the best night of my life and one I won't ever forget. But the morning after left a lot to be desired."

"What happened?"

Dee sighed deeply. "Guilt set in on his part. I saw it in his eyes, all over his face. He wouldn't even look at me. He told me that we'd made a huge mistake. That it should never have happened."

Dee didn't say anything for a long moment, then continued. "I thought he needed time and would eventually come around, but he never did. He avoided me like the plague after that. Then three months later, you came home and announced he'd accepted a job offer in Phoenix. A part of me knew he'd done that to get away from me."

So many times, Dee had thought about reaching out to Cohen, to let him know that he didn't have to do anything as drastic as move away. But a part of her resented his decision to put so much distance between them.

"I admit, at the time, I couldn't believe he was leaving Memphis," Stacey said, breaking into her thoughts. "But I didn't think much about it because the job was a great opportunity for him," Stacey said.

Dee nodded. "Yes, but Cohen would not have left, leaving you behind, had it not been for me. And then, when that incident happened between you and Wallace, and you left Memphis to join Cohen in Phoenix, I felt he blamed me. He probably figured that if he'd been in Memphis to protect you, you would never have gotten involved with Wallace in the first place."

Stacey waved off her words. "I would have dated Wallace and he and Gail would have screwed around on me regardless. I believe that time in my life was meant to happen. Had I married Wallace, I would not have met Eli."

Dee knew that to be true. The Wallace Flowers incident had definitely spurred Stacey on to make some changes. "But still, for the longest time, I felt guilty for being the reason Cohen left Memphis."

She took another sip of her drink. "Although I knew I was probably the last person Cohen wanted to see, I loved coming to see you. You are my best friend—there was no way I wasn't going to visit you. Still, I don't know if you noticed, but he made himself scarce whenever I came to town."

"Yes, but the two of you looked pretty cozy at his going-away party. I know you left with him that night."

"Yes. That was the second time I managed to seduce him. But like before, he said sleeping with me had been a mistake. That's why I returned to Memphis earlier than planned."

"I'm sorry, Dee."

"Don't be. I brought it all on myself. Cohen let the ten-year difference in our ages get in the way. Personally, I don't believe it. I just don't think he finds me attractive."

Stacey snorted. "If he hadn't found you attractive, he would not have slept with you in the first place."

"Then what do you think, Stace? At my parents' anniversary party, he tried avoiding me. And when I cornered him on the terrace, we had words. I told him that I hoped he had a long and miserable life. At the time, I meant it. Then weeks later, I saw him at your wedding and..."

"And what?"

"I decided that I didn't want Cohen to have a miserable life. I want him to be happy. So I've moved on. It was hard, but I'm not going to give Cohen the chance to hurt me again."

"When was the last time you saw him?" Stacey asked.

"Not since your wedding."

"That long ago? It's been well over two years."

"I know, but I felt I needed the time to get over him."

"And have you?"

"Yes. Rejection hurts and I'm not a masochist. At some point, a girl has to decide when she's had enough." Dee refused to love a man who evidently didn't want it. So she'd dated a bit, but so far, hadn't met anyone who held her interest.

"At least I don't have to worry about seeing him at Eli's party. Thanks for letting me know that he won't be there," Dee said.

"Umm...I forgot to mention, those plans have changed."

Dee felt her heartbeat jump. "What do you mean?"

"Cohen will be coming after all. In fact, he arrived earlier today. He's here in Phoenix."

**

"What about you, Cohen? You in?"

Cohen took another sip of his beer as glanced across the room at Zion Blackstone. Zion, who'd until recently been living in Rome, was a friend of the Steele brothers. Zion was also an internationally renowned jeweler. Cohen shook his head. "No, I'll pass."

"You sure?"

"Positive." Zion was soliciting members for the Guarded Hearts Club. To become a member of this single guys club, where no married men were allowed, you had to take a pledge to remain a bachelor. Although Cohen didn't intend to ever marry, he still didn't want to belong to any club. Besides, from what he'd seen, the group wasn't particularly effective. Most of the men who'd pledged never to marry, had. Then they'd dropped out of the club, which was why Zion, the lone member, was now desperately recruiting new comrades.

Zion shifted his gaze from Cohen to Gannon Steele, the youngest of the Steele brothers and the one Cohen knew was the most impressionable. "What about you, Gannon? You in?"

Gannon's smile was huge. Anyone would think someone had offered him the key to a brothel in Las Vegas. "Hell, yeah, I'm in. And I know five other guys who might be interested, as well."

"That's great!" Zion said. "When can I meet them?"

"Tomorrow night. They're coming with me to Eli's birthday party."

Eli frowned at Gannon. "Hey, wait a minute. They weren't invited to my party. They're *your* friends, not mine."

"I asked Stacey if I could invite them. She said yes."

Eli stared at Gannon as if he wanted to strangle him.

Cohen couldn't help but grin. When he'd moved to Phoenix five years ago, he hadn't known a soul. But on his first day at the hospital, he'd met Tyson Steele, another surgeon. They had immediately hit it off, and quickly became the best of friends.

Tyson had a personality that made people let their guard down. He was a dedicated surgeon who always put his patients first. But outside the hospital, he was very different. Before settling down and getting married last year, Tyson had been the ultimate ladies' man, one who never got tired of the thrill of the chase.

"Want another beer?" Tyson asked him, interrupting his thoughts.

"No, I'm fine."

"You're quiet," Tyson said, his green eyes sharp with concern.

"I've got a lot on my mind," Cohen said, before taking a swig of his beer.

"Work?"

"No, personal."

Tyson nodded, and then downed a mouthful of his own beer. Cohen knew his best friend would leave it at that. Tyson always respected his privacy. He knew that if there was anything Cohen needed to talk about, he'd eventually get it off his chest.

"How's married life going?" he asked Tyson.

Tyson smiled. "I never thought I'd say this, but married life is wonderful. I can't imagine a life without Hunter in it." He put his beer bottle to his lips and took another swallow. "You sure you don't want to crash at my place instead of that hotel, Cohen? You know you're welcome."

Cohen nodded. "Thanks, but you and Hunter are still practically newlyweds. You need your privacy." He knew he could have stayed with Tyson or his sister, but had declined both invitations, and checked into a hotel, instead. He had to prepare himself for when he saw Dee. It would be the first time their paths had crossed in two and a half years.

At first, he'd taken the coward's way out and told Stacey he couldn't make it. But the more he thought about it, the more he decided not to let Dee's presence be a factor. He couldn't avoid her forever. Besides, he planned to attend her brother Lawyer's wedding next month, so he'd have to see her then. She was his sister's best friend and their paths would likely cross many times in the years to come.

He figured that he might as well bite the bullet now, accepting how things were and how they would always be.

2

Cohen was in Phoenix... Dee tried her best to put the thought out of her mind but couldn't. She and Stacey had decided to go shopping and instead of concentrating on finding something to wear to the party tomorrow night, her mind was consumed with thoughts of him, the man she'd tried so hard to get over.

"Found anything you like yet?" Stacey asked.

"Not yet, but I see that you have," she said, glancing at the outfits Stacey had across her arm.

"Yes. I'm going in the dressing room to try these on. By the way, Brittany called. She, Hunter and Nikki are in the area shopping as well. I invited them to join us for dinner later. I hope that's okay."

Brittany was married to Galen Steele. Nikki was married to Jonas Steele and Hunter had married Tyson Steele--who was Cohen's best friend--nine months ago. "That's fine. It'll be fun." And it would give her the chance to finally meet Hunter. Stacey had been going on and on about what a nice person she was.

"I'm sure you'll find something for the party," Stacey said over her shoulder as she headed toward the dressing room.

"I just need to keep looking," Dee assured her. *That is, if I can keep my mind off Cohen.* He didn't deserve her interest, so why was he getting it?

"May I help you?"

Obviously, Stacey wasn't the only one who'd noticed Dee's preoccupation. A salesgirl who barely looked a day over twenty had come to help her out. "I'm looking for a party dress."

"How daring?"

Dee lifted a brow. "How daring?"

"Yes, how much skin do you want to show?"

Typically, Dee dressed conservatively—after all, she was usually in a classroom--but she didn't have a problem wearing something sexy now and then. "Do you have any outfits that push the envelope?"

The younger woman nodded with a huge smile. "Yes. And I can think of a few that will look great on you."

Umm, pushing the envelope might not be such a bad idea, especially since Cohen would be at the party. She had no problem showing him exactly what he'd turned down. "Then please show me what you have."

**

Several hours later, Dee and Stacey walked into Maxell's, a popular restaurant in town for evening dining. Dee had ended up purchasing two outfits—she hadn't been able to make up her mind which one she liked best.

"There they are," Stacey said excitedly, waving at the three women sitting at a table that had a view of the mountains.

Hugs were exchanged all around and finally, Dee was introduced to Hunter. She liked Tyson Steele's wife immediately.

"So where are the twins?" Dee asked Brittany. Galen and Brittany had one-year-old twins, an adorable boy and girl.

Brittany smiled. "They are spending time with my in-laws. Drew and Eden are the greatest! They love being grandparents. I have a feeling I'm going to have to watch that they don't spoil the twins rotten."

Dee smiled. She'd met Drew and Eden Steele. All six of the Steele brothers had inherited Eden's beautiful green eyes. Eden was a former international fashion model whose face had graced the covers of several magazines, the likes of Vogue and Elle.

"I love your hair," Nikki said to Dee. "You have the perfect face for that style."

A smile touched Dee's lips. "Thanks." She'd received a lot of compliments since she bitten the bullet and got her hair cut, leaving it short and curly. It was just the carefree style she needed for the summer months.

After the waiter brought out glasses of water and took their dinner orders, Brittany asked Stacey, "Everything all set for the party tomorrow?"

A huge smile covered Stacey's lips. "Yes. I spoke with the caterer today to finalize the food menu."

Dee took a sip of her water and listened to the conversation around her. It was easy to see the bonds between the women. Although she hadn't yet seen Tyson and Hunter together, there wasn't any doubt in her mind that the Steele brothers adored the women they'd married. Some women, she thought, had all the luck.

She had to believe that one day, she'd find her happily ever after. A vision of Cohen flashed in her mind and she quickly forced it back out. He'd had his chance with her. She only hoped that one day, he would realize just what he'd thrown away.

**

Cohen entered his hotel room. He had enjoyed hanging out with friends. Back in Florida, he'd met a lot of good guys at the hospital, but he hadn't struck up a close friendship with any of them. And as far as dating went, he'd been out a few times, but truthfully, he hadn't been interested in a woman since making love to Dee.

He doubted he would ever forget the night he'd first noticed Deidre Lewis was no longer a kid. He had been passing through Columbus and dropped by the apartment that Stacey shared with Dee while attending Ohio State University. Stacey hadn't been home, but a twenty-year old Dee was, and she was just about to go out to a party. She had looked good. Too good. She was dressed differently than he'd ever seen her. Gone was the t-shirt, jeans and sneakers he was used to seeing on her. That night, he'd thought she was showing way too much skin with the short dress that had a cut-out at her stomach that proudly displayed a belly-ring. But what had really caught his attention were the legs that seemed to go on forever and the pair of stilettos on her feet. He'd been speechless.

She had invited him to hang around while she finished getting dressed since Stacey was on her way back home. By finishing, he'd hoped Dee had meant she would either be changing her outfit or covering up all that exposed skin. She'd done neither. In fact, she had spent ten minutes in her bedroom doing something he thought was way too sexy-looking to her hair. By the time Stacey returned home, he had felt as if he needed a stiff drink.

From that night on, he'd become even more aware of Dee. And he didn't like it. He had tried putting distance between them but that was hard to do, considering she was Stacey's best friend. He suddenly remembered the time Dee's parents and brothers had gone on a cruise and left a sick Dee behind. Stacey and Dee had moved back to Memphis after college and were sharing an apartment. During this particular time, Stacey had been in Dallas at an International Technology convention, but she'd called and asked him to drop by the house to check on a sick Dee.

Dee had managed to drag herself to the door, then had practically passed out at his feet. She'd been burning up with a fever. The doctor in him had kicked in and he had carried her into her bedroom, put her back to bed and had spent the next twenty-four hours working to get her temperature down and get liquids into her dehydrated body. He'd refused to leave her, until Stacey had arrived the next day.

Cohen had seen Dee two weeks later, when she'd shown up at his apartment to thank him. Though he'd told her there was no need, she'd insisted and entered carrying bags of groceries. To show her appreciation, she'd intended to make his favorite dish, a pot of seafood gumbo.

He still wasn't sure which had gotten to him first, the thought of eating gumbo or the fact that she'd shown up wearing a halter top, a pair of shorts that should have been outlawed and a pair of stilettos. The shoes were red with gray wiggly lines on the back and heel. He couldn't help noticing, again, that Dee had the legs for them.

Against his better judgement, he had let her stay, thinking he would just ignore her, reading his medical journals, while she worked. But it was hard to ignore a woman who'd taken over his kitchen as if it had been her own. And watching her move around in those shorts and high heels had nearly driven him crazy.

He hadn't counted on her hanging around to eat with him, but would admit it had been nice sharing a meal with her. He'd found out that she liked kids, which was why she'd gone for a degree in education. She also had plans to return to college for her Master's degree and was even tossing around the idea of getting a PhD. He was a big supporter of higher education and had applauded her for considering the idea.

Before leaving, she had insisted on helping him with the dishes and that's when it had happened. While removing the plates from the table, their hands had touched. The next thing he knew, he'd lowered his mouth to hers in a kiss. Even now, the memory made him feel hot all over.

That single kiss had lasted way too long, and had awakened his senses, completely removing his blinders where Dee was concerned. But the thought of a thirty-two-year-old man lusting after a twenty-two-year-old woman had bothered him. He'd finally ended the kiss. But all the apologies he'd made afterwards couldn't erase the taste of her from his mouth.

Dee had waved off his apology, then told him something that had stopped him in his tracks. She had licked her lips as if he'd left behind the sweetest of tastes and looked him in the eyes. Then she'd said that she'd loved him forever and intended to marry him one day.

Her words had shocked the hell out of him. He'd told her that such a thing wasn't possible and had asked her to leave. Acting as if she hadn't been bothered by his rebuff, she had strutted out of the kitchen on those stilettos, grabbed her purse off the living room table and given him an *I-will-be-back* smile before leaving.

As he began stripping off his clothes to take a shower, he wished he had taken her words as a warning. Because three months later, Dee had come back. And she'd seduced the hell out of him.

3

"Will you please stop looking at yourself as if you're naked?"

Dee glanced up at Stacey. "I can't help it. I feel naked," she said, looking down at her outfit again. She'd worn skimpy clothes before, but none this daring. It hadn't looked so scanty when she'd tried it on in the store. She hadn't imagined the flesh-tone material would blend in so perfectly with her skin, to the point that it was almost see-through in certain parts... Or at least, it gave the illusion that it was. And to top it off, she was wearing a pair of shiny chocolate brown stilettos.

"You look gorgeous and your makeup is flawless. And I agree with Nikki. That short and curly hairstyle looks fabulous on you."

"Thanks. You're sure I look okay?"

"Positive. However, your fretting makes me wonder."

Dee lifted an arched brow. "About what?"

"If there's someone coming tonight you want to impress."

"There isn't," she said almost too quickly and wished she hadn't. Dee took a deep breath. "So what if Cohen is coming tonight?"

"I didn't mention my brother's name, Dee."

"You didn't have to. I know that look."

Stacey smiled. "Do you?"

"Yes. And what you're thinking isn't true. If anything, I'm looking forward to meeting some of the single men there."

"Cohen is single."

"Then let me rephrase that. Single men who aren't Cohen. Maybe I didn't make myself clear at lunch, but your brother means nothing to me anymore. I walked away a long time ago, my pride intact," she said, following Stacey, who was moving around, conducting last minute checks on everything. People would begin arriving at any moment.

Trying to forget Cohen hadn't been easy. In the past couple of years, she'd gone back to school and had gotten a Master's degree at night while teaching school during the day. She'd recently been selected to teach third grade at another school, one with a stellar reputation. Now she was considering working on her PhD. As for dating, she'd gone out when it suited her, though she found herself comparing the guys to Cohen. The ones her age seemed immature, so she'd started dating men at least five years older than her. That hadn't worked out either—a lot of them were too bossy and set in their ways.

As she followed Stacey, she admired her friend's beautiful home. Stacey and Eli had built it a few months ago and this would be their first party since moving in. The house sat on three acres of land and was massive--the perfect size for the huge family they wanted to have one day.

Stacey owned a gift shop on the main floor of the Steele Building in downtown Phoenix. The building was owned by Eli. Dee thought her best friend had always been talented when it came to decorating, and her gift showed tonight. Caterers were handling the food but the decorating had all been done by Stacey and her appointed committee of friends.

"So, who are the single guys, other than Cohen, that are coming tonight?" Dee asked curiously.

Stacey glanced at her and smiled. "You know Eli's two single brothers, Mercury and Gannon. They'll be here. Then there's the Steele brothers' friend, Zion. You know him as well. Gannon is bringing five other friends who I haven't met yet. And Eli has invited several single friends, as well, though some of them are bringing dates."

The doorbell rang and Stacey checked her watch and smiled. "Looks like the first of our guests has arrived."

**

Cohen released a deep breath, half-listening to the conversation between the men standing around him. It was hard to pay attention to what they were saying while trying to keep Dee within his sight. She hadn't so much as looked his way. He wished he could be as detached.

He'd caught sight of her the minute he walked into the house. His jaw nearly dropped to the floor when he'd seen her outfit. Why in the world would she wear something like that? Something guaranteed to grab attention? Granted, she looked good in it, but that was beside the point. And what had she done with her hair? The short, curly cut made her look too damn sexy for her own good.

Cohen couldn't help noticing that the guys Gannon had brought with him to the party were hanging all over her, practically breathing down her neck. And dammit, she was letting them.

"Hey man, you okay?"

Cohen glanced over at Tyson. "I'm fine. It's just…"

Tyson lifted a brow. "It's just what?"

"Nothing." He took a sip of his beer and glanced around the room. When he saw Stacey, he knew what he had to do. "Excuse me for a minute," he said to Tyson. "I need to talk to Stacey about something."

He moved across the room to where Stacey was welcoming a couple of late arrivals. "Got a minute?" he asked her.

She smiled up at him. "Sure. What's up?"

Cohen tried to steady his breathing as he noticed one of Gannon's friends lean in so close to Dee that their lips nearly touched. "Damn."

"Cohen? Are you okay?"

He swiped a hand down his face. No, he wasn't okay. Not when he wanted to cross the room and smash the guy's face in. "Can we go somewhere and talk privately?"

"Sure. Come on. We can use one of the guest bedrooms."

He followed his sister down a hall to where her guest bedrooms were located. They entered one and she closed the door behind them. "Cohen? What's going on?"

"You tell me. What's up with Dee? Did you see what she's wearing?"

Stacey raised a brow. "Yes. In fact, I was with her yesterday when she bought it. I think she looks fine. Not everyone can pull an outfit like that off. She has both the body and the legs for it."

He didn't need anyone to tell him about Dee's body and legs. He was pretty damn familiar with both. He had kissed that body all over and had found heaven between those legs. "Whether she looks good in that outfit or not is beside the point."

"Oh? And what *is* the point, Cohen? Dee is single, beautiful, smart and intelligent. She's not hurting anyone with how she chose to dress tonight. I think the outfit looks very flattering on her."

"Well, I don't."

Stacey stared at him. "Why?"

When he didn't say anything, she said, "For crying out loud, Cohen. I hope you're not reverting back to your big-brother mode. The one you would try pulling on us when Dee and I were teens. You were worse than Justice ever was. Take a good look at Dee. She's not a kid any longer. She's a twenty-seven-year-old woman. A *single* twenty-seven-year-old woman. She works hard as a teacher and deserves to have fun whenever she likes and with whomever she likes."

"I'm not trying to play the role of big brother," he snapped.

"Then what role have you taken up? Jealous lover, maybe?"

He blinked. For the first time, he wondered how much Stacey knew. She was Dee's best friend, after all. Had Dee told her anything? Did she know what he and Dee had shared? "Jealous lover? What makes you think that?"

"Forget I said that."

No, he couldn't forget it. She knew more than she was admitting to. "You know about me and Dee." It was a statement, not a question.

She nodded. "Yes, she told me. But before you get all huffy, she just told me at lunch yesterday, Cohen. She felt I deserved to know why you've been avoiding her. Don't think I haven't noticed."

"What's between me and Dee is complicated."

"Funny you should say that. I got the distinct feeling from Dee that there's nothing between you two now. She said that you made sure she knew that--"

"I'm ten years older than her, Stacey." Although that wasn't his main concern, it was a safe one, one he could tell people. To this day, he hadn't revealed what had happened during his disastrous affair with Amanda Forrestal to anyone.

"And Eli is eight years older than me," Stacey said, interrupting his thoughts. "Dad was twelve years older than Mom. Mr. Lewis is eleven years older than Mrs. Lewis. You'll have to do better than that, Cohen. I know you. There is something else. But if you don't want to tell me what it is, that's fine. Still, I think you owe it to Dee to tell her...if you want there to be something between you."

"I don't."

"Then I suggest you not concern yourself about Dee, what she wears and what she does. She wants the same thing most women want."

"And what's that?"

"A man who will appreciate her. Love her. Marry her. What woman doesn't deserve that?"

Marry? The thought of Dee getting serious about anyone twisted his gut. "And she thinks the guys who have been buzzing around her all night are interested in marriage? Guys who happen to be new recruits in that damn Guarded Hearts Club Zion is expanding?"

Stacey shrugged. "I don't know anything about that, since I just met them for the first time tonight. But Dee is getting to know them. And once they get to know her, I believe they'll find out what a wonderful person she is." She reached out and patted him on the arm. "Don't let it bother you that marriage is probably the last thing on those guys' minds. Eli would confess to the same thing when he met me. Some women can change a man's heart."

"And some men can break a woman's heart, Stacey."

"How well I know, thanks to Wallace. But in the end, he unknowingly did me a favor." She turned to listen to the party going on downstairs. "I need to run. You going to be okay?"

He nodded. "Go ahead. I'll be down in a minute."

After Stacey left, Cohen thought about what she'd said. Was he acting the part of a jealous lover? He knew he had no right. He'd made it as plain as he could to Dee that there could never be anything between them. He'd known his words had hurt, but he hadn't wanted her to think seducing him would eventually make him fall in love with her. There was no way for that to happen.

Like he'd told Stacey, men could break a woman's heart. But a woman could also break a man's. Like Amanda had broken his.

He was convinced that he had fallen in love with Amanda the first time he'd laid eyes on her, his first day in biology class at Harvard. For months, she had led him to believe the feelings were mutual. He'd had no idea some women could be so deceitful. While in high school, he hadn't dated much, since he needed top marks to get into pre-med at Harvard. If he had, maybe he wouldn't have been so blindsided by Amanda. He'd have understood that all women were not the same, that some had not-so-pure motives for seeking a man out, that some would feign interest until someone they felt was a better catch came along.

Unfortunately for him, he'd found out what a phony she was during what was the worst period in his life. He'd gotten word from his mom that he needed to come home immediately because his father had been injured in a job-related accident. Within twenty-four hours of Cohen's arrival in Memphis, his father had been gone.

He had tried contacting Amanda to let her know about his father, but hadn't been able to reach her. Nor had she returned any of his calls.

When he returned to school weeks later, he'd discovered that she'd taken up with a guy in law school, the son of a senator with his eye on politics. When Cohen had questioned her about it, she had laughed in his face, telling him she'd rather be a senator's wife than a mere doctor's.

Amanda's betrayal, combined with the grief of losing his father pushed him into an abyss of depression, one so deep he thought he'd never manage to climb back out. He hadn't had any close friends to help him through it and his mother, Stacey and his father's sister, Aunt Maggie, had been going through their own grief. He couldn't burden them with his, too.

All he'd had was a heart filled with pain and despair. He'd skipped classes and was on the verge of flunking out the semester and losing all his scholarships. There were days when he refused to talk to anyone, even his roommate. The pain overwhelmed him. He'd even thought about lashing out in some of the craziest, most self-destructive ways. He just hadn't cared any more.

Luckily for him, someone had cared. One of his professors, Dr. Dahl, had recognized the signs of depression and had reached out to him. The man had encouraged him to get help and had even put him in contact with a psychiatrist off campus, who as a favor to Dr. Dahl, would treat him for free. It had been years later that Cohen had discovered those sessions with the psychiatrist hadn't been free, at all. Dr. Dahl had footed the bill for all of them.

Cohen drew in a deep breath. That period of time had been what he termed as the "black hole" in his life. When he loved, he loved hard. He couldn't risk falling into that hole for a second time. His heart and his sanity couldn't take it.

He was well aware he was attracted to Dee. Hell, what man wouldn't be? She was an extremely beautiful woman.

Intelligent. And she had a heart of gold, just like his sister. He'd always thought Dee and Stacy balanced each other.

Once he'd started looking at Dee with different eyes, that attraction had only grown. And once he'd had her in his bed, he couldn't lose the memory of what it was like to kiss her. Touch her. Taste her all over. Be inside of her.

Even with the distance between them, he couldn't forget her. He'd still think of her, long for her, wake up with memories of the times he'd had her. How she had given herself to him in a way that, even now, made him wish…

Cohen shook his head. He couldn't wish. He couldn't imagine and he needed to stop fantasizing. Dee deserved better. She deserved more than he could ever give.

Accepting that as final, he turned and left the guest bedroom.

4

The clinking of a knife against a wine glass had everyone glancing toward the center of the room.

"May I have everyone's attention?" Stacey stood there smiling excitedly. "It's time to cut the cake. Can we all gather out on the patio to wish Eli a 'Happy Birthday'?"

Dee refused to let her gaze seek Cohen out. She'd seen enough of him when he'd arrived. The air she'd been breathing had seemed to shift in the room, getting charged from his presence. She'd always thought Stacey's brother was larger than life and tonight was no exception. He was tall, tempting and tantalizing.

She had been standing in the entryway between the kitchen and dining room when he had strode into the house. Although she'd had a good view of him, he hadn't been able to see her. But she didn't have to be standing directly in front of Cohen to be overwhelmed by his presence. Those whiskey colored eyes beneath a dark slash of brows, his creamy brown complexion, his short hair, perfectly sculpted chin, full lips and the signature sexy-looking, five o'clock shadow on his jaw were the same ones he had when he came to her in her dreams. All in all, he was just too handsome for words.

Forcing thoughts of Cohen from her mind, she tried focusing on what Midas Coronado was saying. They'd all sang happy birthday to Eli and were now eating slices of cake. Midas, a friend of Gannon's, was nice enough, definitely good looking and was part of the mega-wealthy family that owned the international Coronado Tire Company. She wondered if, like the Greek King he'd told her that his parents named him for, he thought he had the Midas touch, turning everything to gold. One thing for certain, if he lacked the touch, he definitely knew how to wield the *Midas charm.* He was pouring it on thick tonight.

The fact that Midas was a ladies' man didn't bother her. The words were all but tattooed on his forehead for all to see. He was no different than his other friends who'd hit on her tonight. She could handle them. In fact, she was enjoying having them compete for her attention. She understood how the male mind worked. After all, she had two brothers, who for the longest time, had assumed they were God's gift to women. At least Lawyer had come to his senses and settled down. Somehow though, she couldn't see Justice getting serious with a woman anytime soon.

"So, how long will you be in Phoenix?" he asked as they, along with the others, began moving back inside.

Dee glanced up at Midas. "I fly out Tuesday."

"So what are your plans for Memorial Day?"

She wondered why he wanted to know. "Eli's parents host an annual cookout. I'll be going with Stacey and Eli."

"I heard about that party. Gannon invited me. Wasn't sure I was going to go, but maybe now I will."

Dee chose to ignore Midas's insinuation that her presence at the Steele's cookout was a deciding factor. "So how did you and Gannon meet?"

"Business deals. His family's freight company transports a lot of our products to other states."

Dee was aware that Eli's father owned a huge shipping company and that Gannon was the only one of the six Steele sons who'd followed their father into that business. While Midas continued to tell her about his and Gannon's friendship, she caught sight of Cohen out of the corner of her eye. He was talking to Eli's parents.

"You know Dee, we can do something to get that guy in the dark slacks and grey shirt to notice us, if that's what you want."

Dee blinked at Midas. "Excuse me."

A smile touched his lips. "I am a very perceptive man. Although you've pretended to hang on to my every word, I know that your attention has been elsewhere. Mainly on that guy Gannon introduced me to earlier, Dr. Cohen Carlson."

Had she been that obvious? She could say she didn't know what Midas was talking about, but she refused to insult his intelligence that way. If he had picked up on her interest in Cohen, then he was a very perceptive man. "I owe you an apology."

"Not really. A person can't always control the workings of their heart."

His words gave her pause. It sounded like he spoke from experience. "Some things aren't meant to be, no matter how we wish otherwise."

"I agree. You're a beautiful woman and he was a fool to let you go," Midas responded.

She smiled up at him, tempted to admit that Cohen had never truly wanted her in the first place. "It's not that big of a deal, honestly," she said.

He chuckled. "You know one of the things I like about you Dee?"

"What? That I don't lie very well?" she asked in a teasing tone.

He chuckled again. "No, I get the impression that you're dedicated to any cause you're excited about. Whether it's the kids you teach...or a past love you're trying to let go of."

Past love she was trying to let go of? She could honestly say she'd thought she'd already managed to do that.

"Well, I've dominated your attention enough for tonight," Midas said, reaching out and giving her hand a tight, affectionate squeeze before letting it go. "Hopefully once I back off, your guy will stop staring holes in my back and make his move."

Make his move? Honestly. She'd given Cohen plenty of opportunities to do that. Still, what had Midas said about Cohen staring holes in his back? That couldn't be right.

**

Out of the corner of his eye, Cohen saw the man who'd dominated Dee's attention all evening walk away. Great! She was finally alone so he could at least speak to her. It had been over two years and there was no reason they couldn't go back to being friends, now that they understood each other.

Without wasting any time, in case the dude returned, he swiftly crossed the room to Dee. The closer he got, the more he had to admit how good she looked in that outfit and those stilettos. Although he wished she wasn't getting so much male attention… Still, he was forced to admit that seeing that outfit on any other woman probably would not have bothered him so much. The fact that it was Dee who was wearing it, though, did bother him…and that realization annoyed the hell out him.

Then there was her new hairstyle. In all the years he'd known her, she'd never worn her hair short. It would take some getting used to but he had to admit the style looked good on her, and those huge dangling earrings gave it a wow effect.

She glanced over at him and saw his approach. He could feel her apprehension. It bothered him that things were this way between them. She was erecting a wall around herself. But then, hadn't he done the same with her? "Hello Dee," he said.

"Cohen."

"Nice party." He was standing close enough to inhale her scent. He knew this particular cologne had been her favorite for years and he hoped she never changed it.

"Yes, Stacey did a great job."

"I understand you helped out a lot."

She smiled and the way her lips parted had his gut clenching. "Stace would claim that. I merely came up with ideas for the decorations."

He glanced around. Anyone knowing Eli was aware of how serious he was most of the time. They also knew he loved football and his favorite team was the Arizona Cardinals. Cohen figured that was the reason behind the sports theme of the party. The only thing Eli loved more than the Cardinals was his wife. "Well, I think it's a great party and I love the decorations, especially this," he said, pulling a Cardinal referee whistle from his pocket.

Cohen couldn't decide what had delighted Eli the most. Hearing the sound of the cardinals all over the house, or the sight of his frat brothers performing a two-step in the middle of the floor just after they all arrived.

He glanced back at Dee, studying her features. "I like your hair, by the way."

"Thanks. It will be easier to manage over the summer while school is out."

"You're not teaching this summer?" He knew that even when the school term was over, she taught reading at a number of senior citizen centers around Memphis. She'd been doing so for years, even before graduating from college.

"No, I've decided to take a break and do something fun for a change."

Do something fun? He wondered what that was. Before he could ask, even though he probably didn't have the right, Stacey got everyone's attention again.

"Hi everyone. I'm about to present Eli with his birthday gift. I hope he likes it."

Eli leaned over and kissed Stacey on the cheek before accepting the huge box from her. Cohen and everyone else figured things out the moment Eli unwrapped the gift to expose a huge box of disposable diapers. Eli, however, just stood there, as if stunned. Then he turned to Stacey with a huge grin on his face. "Does this mean what I think it does?" he asked her.

Tears misted Stacey's eyes as she nodded. "Yes. We're having a baby, Eli."

Eli let out a huge cheer before pulling Stacey into his arms, kissing her soundly in front of everyone. A lot of clapping and even more cardinal sounds from the whistles, followed. Cohen glanced over at Dee and saw tears in her eyes. "You knew already, didn't you?" he said.

She nodded. "Yes. Stacey told me the minute I got into town. Just think Cohen. You're going to be an uncle and I'll be a godmother."

He was thinking about it and he was so filled with happiness that he wanted to pull Dee into his arms, but knew he couldn't. That's how things had become messed up between them at his going-away party two years ago.

He glanced over. Eli had finally released Stacey. And just as Cohen had thought, his sister's gaze sought him out. He crossed the room to give Stacey a huge hug. "The folks would have been ecstatic. Just think. You're carrying their first grandchild," he whispered.

Stacey wiped tears from her eyes. "I know and I am so happy about it." Then in a quieter tone, she added, "You know, you should have done the honors. You're the oldest."

"It won't ever happen," he said quickly. But upon seeing that concerned look in his sister's eyes, he added, "Besides, you'll wear motherhood a lot better than I could ever wear fatherhood."

He then pulled Stacey into his arms for another huge hug. But he felt a trickle of unease slide down his spine. Looking up, he soon saw the cause. Midas Coronado was back at Dee's side.

5

Dee pulled herself up in bed, too excited to sleep. After Stacey's announcement, it quickly became evident to everyone that Eli was ready for the party to end so he could have his wife all to himself.

In a way, Dee felt bad because she was staying with them. But when she'd suggested getting a hotel for the night, Stacey had just laughed at her. Eli and Stacey's home was huge. Dee practically had her own wing, which was on the other side of the house from the master suite. So it wasn't as if she was in their way.

She knew Stacy and Eli had been waiting until they'd settled into their new home before they started a family. And they definitely hadn't wasted any time. Just seeing the once womanizing Steele brothers tonight, noticing how they doted on their wives, made Dee believe there was still hope. One day, she would meet a man who would truly love her.

Her thoughts shifted to Cohen.

Getting out of bed, she walked over to the window and glanced out at the mountains. In the past, she and Cohen had tried avoiding each other, but tonight they'd shared words. He had been standing close to her, so close that she'd caught the scent of his aftershave. She'd been able to study the shape of his mouth up close, and had been bombarded by the memories of the feel of his lips on hers.

Although she and Cohen hadn't spoken after Stacey's announcement, she'd known each and every time he'd glanced over at her. Her body had responded in full awareness. At one point, she'd even felt her nipples swell and tingle. When she'd glanced over at him, he'd held her gaze for only a moment before looking away.

She couldn't help wondering if he was thinking of the times they'd been intimate. How he'd let himself go, touched her all over, tasted every single spot on her body…made love to her like he hadn't wanted to stop. Ever. Or was he remembering the mornings after…when the guilt had set in? When he'd retreated as if it was the right thing to do? The only thing to do.

Drawing in a deep breath she pressed her forehead against the window pane and closed her eyes, remembering that first night with Cohen, nearly five years ago…

GUILTY PLEASURE

Dee nervously entered Cohen's apartment, closed the door behind her and leaned against it, releasing a deep breath. She was convinced she was doing the right thing. One of them had to make the first move and since he wouldn't, she was picking up the slack.

He'd tried hiding his attraction to her but she could see it, sense it. And she had no intention of taking it easy on him, now that she knew he wanted her as much as she wanted him. It was there in his eyes whenever he looked at her. The heat. The fire. And her body had responded. It had gotten so bad that all Stacey had to do was mention her brother and Dee's nipples would harden.

In her mind, she'd relived the kiss they'd shared a few months ago. She couldn't put it out of her mind. And the memories of it caused an indescribable ache within her.

She glanced at her watch. Over the phone, Cohen had told Stacey that he'd be back by nine-thirty. Which meant that he would be home in less than an hour. There was no time to lose. Moving quickly, she headed for his bedroom.

It didn't take her long to strip down to nothing and slide between the sheets. Then, she waited. No one knew of her plan, not even Stacey. Her best friend would have tried talking her out of this crazy scheme and she refused to let anyone do that. She'd never done anything like this before and wouldn't have felt compelled to do it now if Cohen

54

hadn't been denying the chemistry between them. She knew he thought he was too old for her, but she was ready to defuse that argument.

Tonight, she would prove to him that she was the only woman he needed. Sure, she expected him to put up a fuss, to say there was nothing between them. That's why she'd studied all those books on seduction. Poor Cohen wouldn't know what hit him.

Before going to bed at night, she'd read the books and study all the illustrated pictures. Then, when she fell asleep, she'd dream about Cohen doing all those things to her.

And tonight was the night.

She wasn't sure how long she'd lain there, staring up at the ceiling, when she'd finally heard his key inserted in the door. It was around ten. She held her breath. He was humming. Was that a good sign?

She heard him moving around in the kitchen. Then moments later, she heard the footsteps coming down the hall. Getting closer. And closer. And then she knew he was in the room. Suddenly the ceiling lights went on. He was moving toward the bathroom, when he suddenly turned and stared straight at her.

"What are you doing here, Dee?"

She saw the shock, the outrage on his face. But there was something else, too…

She thought about pulling herself up in bed, then remembered she wasn't wearing any clothes. Not a stitch. He wasn't supposed to find that out until later, although she figured he suspected as much.

"I was waiting for you."

His brow rose. "Waiting for me?" At her nod, he asked. "Why?"

"So you can make love to me."

From the hard expression that suddenly appeared on his features, she knew that had been the wrong answer. Apparently the author of the book she'd read on seduction, the one who claimed men preferred women to be upfront with them, hadn't asked Cohen Carlson.

"You need to leave, Dee."

"Why?"

"Because you have no business being here, let alone making a statement like that."

"Are you going to deny you want me, Cohen?"

"Yes, I'm going to deny it. I can't believe Stacey helped you set this up. Now leave."

"Stacey doesn't know anything about this. But you're right. I have no right to be in your apartment uninvited, but

I came here for a reason. I need you to admit there is something between us."

He shook his head. "Whatever you think is between us is all in your head."

"I refuse to believe that. I see the way you look at me and--"

"And you decided to get into my bed, based on the way I looked at you?"

"Yes. You've done it more than once."

"It means nothing other than I've noticed you're not a kid anymore. And I wouldn't even be noticing, if you wore more clothes and a pair of comfortable shoes instead of those high heels you're so fond of."

"There's nothing wrong with how I dress. My clothes can't be that bad, because I know there were times you couldn't take your eyes off of me."

He rubbed his hand down his face, obviously frustrated with her. "It's all about lust, Dee. Grow up and one day you will understand how a man's mind works."

She lifted her chin. "I already know. I have brothers."

"Please leave, Dee. Either you leave or I will. You are not welcome here."

Dee stared at him. This definitely wasn't going the way she'd expected. In the books, she'd read that a man's usual reaction to finding a naked woman in his bed, was to begin ripping off his clothes. So why was Cohen being so stubborn? He wanted her. She wanted him. What was the problem? "Can we talk?"

"I think you've said enough."

"Can I at least ask you something?" It was something she needed to know.

"What?"

"You are into women, right?" She knew he was into women—why else would he have checked her out so thoroughly and so often? She was merely trying to stall for time, getting him to engage in the conversation he claimed he didn't want to have with her.

He just stared at her. Obviously, he didn't immediately realize what she was asking. Then he hardened his gaze. "Rest assured, I am a heterosexual male. I enjoy women."

She shrugged. "I was just wondering. I've never seen you with one and Stacey never mentioned you being involved with anyone."

He glared down at her. "For your information, my work takes priority over everything in my life right now. And as far as Stacey knowing, I don't necessarily tell her about every single woman I date."

"So you do date?" She wasn't sure she liked hearing that. She much preferred thinking that he didn't.

"Yes, on occasion. When I feel like it. But it's not my top priority. My work as a surgeon is." He glanced at his watch. "Now if you don't mind, I've been on a three hour flight. I'm tired, aggravated and would like to get into my own bed."

"There's enough room for both of us. But if you insist that I leave, then I will." Although she had no intention of doing so. According to one of the books, once a man saw a woman's naked body, that was it! From that moment on, he'd be putty in her hands.

If the man had been anyone other than Cohen--and if she hadn't loved him so much--she wouldn't be doing this. But she'd made up her mind months ago. She wanted him. And she was going to have him. All those sexy items--the shoes, clothes--had been purchased with him in mind.

"Fine. I'll leave."

"Good."

She threw back the covers and slid out of bed in a movement that would have made the most gifted seductress proud. He was seeing it all, just like she wanted him to do. Her breasts, tummy, thighs, legs...and what was between them. And he was looking. If he hadn't wanted to see, he could have turned his back. But he hadn't.

"Please hurry and put on some clothes, Deidre."

Wow. He'd used her full name. This must be serious. She stood beside the bed. "I will. If you truly want me to."

"I truly want you to."

'Okay."

She turned and leaned over to pick up her panties off the floor, deliberately giving him a view of her backside. If he meant for her not to hear his groan, he failed miserably. After skimming her panties up her hips and thighs, she slid her feet into her shoes.

One author had written that men loved a woman's boobs and butt more than anything. But she'd discovered early on that no matter how much cleavage she showed, Cohen's interest was always firmly fastened on her legs. That meant she needed to flaunt what she had and wearing stilettos always did the trick.

"I'll wait in the living room until you finish," he said in a deep guttural tone, as if the words had been forced from his throat.

She glanced over at him. "If that's your desire, Cohen." She clearly saw what he desired from the size of him below his zipper. A man's erection was always a dead giveaway and the book suggested that she keep her eye on the prize. In this case, the big E. In Cohen's case, the massively big E.

He moved toward the door and she wondered if he had the willpower to leave. Regardless of what he said, she could see that he wanted her. Her heart began beating in her chest. Was his willpower stronger than his desire for her?

He was within a foot of the door when he stopped, turned and looked at her with those eyes that made her skin burn. He raked his gaze all over her body—taking in the skimpy pair of panties and red stilettos--before finally zeroing in on her face. His eyes held hers and her heartbeat pounded in her ears. Then he began to slowly walk toward her.

To her, this night would be something special. Cohen wasn't just handsome, he was hers. She loved him. She'd always loved him and was determined that one day, he'd love her too.

When he reached her, he stopped. Then, without saying a word, he leaned in and captured her lips. The moment his mouth touched hers, chills of intense pleasure rippled through Dee's body. They consumed her, making her delirious with desire. She'd known it would be this way. That last kiss had plagued her for weeks, and had been the driving force to this, a repeat performance.

For a man who'd been determined that she leave his apartment a few moments ago, he'd obviously forgotten, because he'd taken control of her mouth. When he deepened the kiss, she had never felt so consumed by a man. And when she felt his hands wrap around her naked middle, to pull her close, the feel of his jeans rubbing against her naked skin was a total turn-on. She moaned and he managed to literally absorb the sound from her lips. His mouth become hungrier, more demanding…devouring.

He suddenly broke off the kiss. She watched through glazed eyes as he tore off his clothes. With each piece he removed and every inch of naked skin exposed, she had to force her breath through her lungs. Cohen Carlson was so perfectly made that she felt an intense drumming start in the lower part of her stomach, just by looking at him. Once he had stripped down completely, he then returned to her. Kneeling, he removed her shoes and then slid her panties back down her legs.

And then he did something she hadn't expected. Something that had never been done to her before. Ever. He leaned in, and easing his mouth between her legs, he devoured her. Right there. She gasped at the contact of his tongue sliding inside of her and grabbed on to his shoulders, to save her from melting to the floor.

He was licking her with an intensity that brought on a moan from deep within her throat. With each stroke of his tongue, she dug her nails into his shoulders. Suddenly, she felt something move within her, beginning at the top of her head and gliding rapidly to the soles of her feet, making her entire body shiver. The tip of his tongue continued to play with her clit, as she moaned and called his name, telling him to stop one minute and go deeper the next.

In response, he jabbed his tongue inside her and did a certain kind of whip-lash movement that had her screaming. An orgasm--her very first man-made one-- ripped through her, wrenching her body as every muscle became tight and rigid. His tongue wasn't through with her yet, though. Its strokes quickened and became even more demanding.

And then suddenly, he withdrew his mouth. Standing, he tumbled her onto the bed. "You tasted so good," he whispered huskily, moving his body over hers.

Honestly, she didn't know what to say to that--no man had ever told her that before. But then, she'd never given one a reason to. Cohen lowered his mouth to hers, kissing her in a way that made her toes curl and ignited sensuous sensations within her all over again, and her mind went blank.

She was so caught up in the kiss that she didn't discern him easing her legs apart until she felt his engorged erection pressing against her womanly folds. She knew she should tell him about her total lack of sexual experience but he'd stop if she did. And she didn't want him to stop. More than anything, she wanted this. She wanted him to be her first...and her last.

Dee felt him ease into her and knew when he detected the barrier telling him it was her first time. He broke off the kiss and stared down at her. She was certain he saw the pain she couldn't hide in her features. Refusing to let him back out, she tightened her legs around his waist and her arms around his neck and forced his mouth back down to hers. She knew he'd given into temptation when he returned her kiss. After a brief moment, the pain of it being her first time began easing away.

He filled her with his full length, then began moving inside of her. He was stroking her into sweet oblivion, setting a rhythm that was driving her mad with desire as pleasurable sensations flitted all through her. This was how it was supposed to be. He was with her and she wanted to believe this was just the beginning.

And then, it happened again. As he kissed her and moved within her, she began trembling as an orgasm took hold. Suddenly, he did something she hadn't expected. He broke off the kiss, threw his head back and screamed her name. *Her name.* Just hearing it from his lips while gripped in the throes of passion pushed her over the edge once more.

At that moment, as his body continued to buck and jerk while thrusting into her wildly, she believed he'd finally accepted what she'd always known. They were meant to be together.

She fell asleep and when she awoke, it was the next day. She opened drowsy eyes to see the brightness of the sun shining in through the window blinds. The first thing she noticed was that she was in bed alone. When she heard a sound, she shifted her gaze from the window to glance across the room. Cohen was fully dressed and sitting in the wingback chair in the corner. He sat staring at her, his legs stretched out and crossed at the ankles.

He had an unreadable expression on his face, but she felt comfortable enough to smile over at him. How could she not, after experiencing such wonderful lovemaking last night. She doubted that she would ever forget how it had felt when he'd exploded inside of her. When he'd broken off their kiss to scream her name. When he'd--

"We should not have done what we did last night, Dee."

His words intruded into her thoughts. She chose to ignore them, smiling as she answered, "It was time that we did, Cohen."

"No. It shouldn't have happened."

"I don't think so. Now stop talking and come back to me. I want you here," she said, patting the empty side of the bed.

He eased up out the chair, his eyes narrowed, his posture rigid and stiff. His hands were tightened into fists, at his sides. "You don't get it, do you?" he said, his tone sharp.

What was there not to get? They'd made beautiful love together. "I don't understand, Cohen?"

"What we did was wrong. You should not have come here. I should not have made love to you."

"But you did. Why are you trippin' about it?" It was quite obvious that he was angry. At her. At himself. At the situation.

"Dammit Dee, I didn't even use a condom."

She waved off his words. "Is that what's got you all upset? Relax. My doctor put me on the pill a few years ago. So as much as I would love to be pregnant, I'm not."

He swore, and then inhaled a deep breath as if he was fighting to control his anger. Obviously, he wasn't getting through to her the way he wanted to do. Again she patted the empty spot beside her. "Come back to bed, Cohen. We can talk later."

He stared at her for a minute and then stepped back. "I need you to get dressed and leave, Dee. Regardless of how you feel about it, what we did was wrong. I should never have touched you. I'm sorry." He shoved his hands into the pockets of his jeans. "I'm leaving for a while. When I get back, I want you gone. I mean it, Dee."

Yes, he meant it, but she needed to know why. "Why are you doing this to us, Cohen?"

"Us?" He chuckled derisively. "There was never an 'us'. Last night we were nothing more than bed partners. You offered something and I took it. I should have refused you. Now I feel guilty as hell."

"Don't feel guilty on my account, Cohen."

"I'm not. I feel bad about what I've done. If you were Stacey, and I found out one of your brothers had done such a thing to her, I would--"

"Mind your own business, I hope. I'm not a child. I am a woman who is old enough to do what I want, with whoever I want. Last night, I wanted you." And then, because she needed him to understand, she added, "I love you."

He looked at her, shocked. "Love me?"

She was disappointed that he'd thought she'd sleep with him without being in love with him. "Yes. I've loved you forever, Cohen."

He shook his head. "Sorry you believe that."

She glared at him. "Don't be sorry. I know my feelings and I do love you."

"In that case, I would advise you not to waste any of your love on me. Give it to someone who deserves you. Someone who can be the person you need. Someone who can love you in return. Because I can't. I don't love you."

Then without saying anything else, he walked out the room. She flinched at the sound of the front door slamming shut behind him.

She stayed there for a few moments after he left, trying to convince herself he hadn't meant what he'd said. But deep down, she knew. Fighting back tears, she got out of bed, put on her clothes and left Cohen's apartment...

Dee opened her eyes, her thoughts returning to the present. She was still in Eli and Stacey's home, standing with her forehead pressed to the window. Remembering her first time with Cohen had brought back painful memories. She recalled going back to her apartment, refusing to give up on him, thinking what he needed was more time. In the meantime, she'd begun dating Eric Stallings, so that it hadn't looked as if she was waiting for him to make a move. Eric was nice enough but her heart belonged to Cohen. Even when he moved to Phoenix, she'd never stopped loving him.

She'd thought that a little time apart might have made him rethink things, that he might have gotten over his inhibitions the night of his going-away party. Again, she and Cohen shared an incredible night. But then, the next morning, the same thing had happened. He'd told her it was a mistake. Totally crushed, she'd taken the first plane home to Memphis.

Now he was here and they were sharing the same air. Two and a half years without seeing him should have destroyed any feelings she had for him. And she'd thought they had. But it had only taken seeing him again tonight, inhaling his scent, feeling his presence, to make all those emotions she had tucked away come rolling back.

The bottom line was…she still loved him, though she wished she didn't. Which meant that she'd have put her heart in lockdown. No matter what she had to do, she wasn't going to let Cohen hurt her again.

6

Cohen was tired of tossing and turning in bed. He knew the reason he couldn't get to sleep. Dee. It had been hard enough to see her tonight, attracting all that male attention in that way-too-sexy outfit and those killer stilettos. But once he'd decided not to avoid her, he couldn't stop his gaze from drifting to her lips. Those same lips he'd enjoyed kissing way too much. He'd felt a sizzle of awareness pass between them.

What the hell was wrong with him, getting all steamed whenever he'd seen her with another man? He should have been glad that she'd finally come to her senses, that she was looking for someone else. And least he didn't have to worry about her pulling some seduction stunt again.

Sitting up in bed, he rubbed a hand down his face. Frustration was setting in again, a common thing whenever he thought of Dee. He'd have thought it would be easier now. After all, it had been more than two years since he'd seen her. But thing's weren't any easier. Why?

After the stunt she'd pulled in Memphis, he hadn't wasted any time accepting a job in Phoenix. It had been his fault. He should have known better, should have handled the situation differently. Instead, he'd behaved like a horny ass and taken what she'd offered, only to regret it the next morning.

Once in Phoenix, he'd tried putting Dee out of his mind. He had struck up a friendship with the Steeles and started a new life. He knew his limitations and made sure he never went beyond them. He'd only dated when it suited him and had shaken his head at the sexual antics of a then-single Tyson. Cohen's best friend had dated enough women for both of them.

But before long, Stacey had moved to Phoenix after breaking up with that lowlife, Wallace. Cohen had been able to avoid Dee's occasional visits to Phoenix, right up until the night of his going away party at Tyson's place. He had been filled with a lot of emotions. The job offer, with its subsequent move to Florida topped the list. It was a dream of a lifetime, but he'd had misgivings about moving and leaving Stacey behind, especially after what had happened when he'd left her in Memphis. But then Eli had announced that he and Stacey had been having this secret affair right under Cohen's nose. They were in love and wanted to get married.

GUILTY PLEASURE

That declaration had dissolved a lot of his concerns and he'd been happy for his sister. Still, he made sure that he and Eli had a one-on-one talk after the party. Afterwards Cohen had been sure that Eli loved his sister and would never break her heart the way Wallace had.

Eli had proposed to Stacey at the party. Dee had been bustling over with happiness and when she'd thrown herself in his arms, he'd forgotten about his decision to keep his distance from her. When the party ended, she'd asked him for a ride back to Stacey's place, since Stacey would be spending the night with Eli. Against his better judgment, he had agreed.

Halfway there, she'd come up with a whole slew of reasons why she didn't want to stay in Stacey's house alone. She'd asked him to take her to his place for the night, offering to sleep on the sofa. Warning bells had sounded in his head. He'd seen the signs that night but had chosen to ignore them. His only defense, if he thought he could claim one, was that Dee had looked damn good that night in a short purple dress and killer stilettos. And he'd have to admit that the sexual awareness between them had been thick enough to cut with a knife.

So, without much resistance, he had taken her to his place with his eyes wide open and his erection hard. The minute he'd closed the door behind them, the battle was lost. All he could think about was having her again. They'd ended up making love until dawn. He could honestly say that Dee was the best sex of his life. Why was he thinking about that now?

His thoughts shifted back to tonight's party. Dee was spending the night with Stacey and Eli, but for all he knew, she could be somewhere with Midas Coronado. Was it any of his business if she was?

Although he didn't ask Stacey, he figured Dee would be flying out sometime tomorrow. He hoped so, especially since he'd made plans to hang around Phoenix for another week or so. Since getting that position at the hospital in Florida, he hadn't really taken any time off. He needed a break.

Cohen couldn't help smiling at the thought of becoming an uncle in around eight months. He'd definitely return to Phoenix to be on hand for that. He wouldn't miss it for the world.

**

"Good morning," Dee said, entering the kitchen to find Stacey and Eli sitting at the table, eating breakfast. She couldn't help noticing the huge smiles on their faces. She didn't have to guess why.

"Good morning, Dee. Sleep well?" Stacey asked, getting up to give her a huge hug.

"Yes, thanks." She patted Stacey's stomach. "I can't believe you have a baby growing inside there. That's pretty friggin' awesome."

"I think so, too," Eli said, smiling broadly, before taking a sip of his coffee. He stood and taking his plate, headed for the sink. "I'm on my way to play a game of basketball with the guys."

Dee knew the "guys" were his brothers and the Steele cousins who'd come to town from North Carolina, as well as a few friends. No doubt Cohen was included, unless he was returning to Florida today. "Have a good game."

He chuckled. "Thanks. I have all the confidence in the world that the Phoenix Steeles will defeat the North Carolina Steeles." Walking back to the table, he gave Stacey a kiss on the lips. "I will see you ladies later, baby."

When he'd left, Stacey glanced over at Dee. "Don't you just love a confident man?"

Dee chuckled as she strolled over to the stove to fill her plate. It had been the aroma of bacon that had awakened her. "Evidently you do."

Stacey's smile widened. "Yes, I do. I truly do."

Dee heard the happiness in Stacey's voice and was happy for her. She deserved it and Dee was grateful that her friend had married into such a wonderful family. Coming to the table to sit down, Dee asked, "So, when is Cohen going back to Florida?" She figured she might as well mention it. The question had been on her mind all morning.

Stacey gazed at her over the rim of her coffee cup. "He hasn't said, but I know it won't be for another week or so. Maybe two."

That surprised Dee. "That long?"

"Yes. Cohen is finally taking a real vacation. He hasn't had one since taking that job in Florida. Now he has no choice. The hospital is making him take the time he's built up. It's their policy."

"Good. He's such a workaholic," Dee said, sprinkling salt onto her eggs.

"He is that. Dedicated to a fault." She gave Dee a sly look. "He noticed your outfit, by the way."

Dee stopped what she was doing and glanced over at Stacey. "Did he?"

"Yes."

"And how do you know?" She tried to slow down the sudden racing of her heart. It shouldn't have mattered one way or the other. But it did.

"Because he hauled me off to the nearest bedroom to read me the riot act. Like I can tell you what or what not to wear. He thought you were showing too much skin. And he didn't like how cozy you were getting with Midas Coronado."

Dee rolled her eyes. "Too bad. Your brother had his chance with me. I'm tired of him sending mixed signals. Typical man."

"Honestly, I'm not sure there's anything typical about this situation. At least not for Cohen. Where you're concerned, I'm positive it's more than the age thing."

Dee lifted a brow. "Then what is it?"

"I truly don't know."

Dee shrugged. "I told you what I thought."

"What? That he doesn't find you attractive enough? That's baloney. In fact, I think he found way too attractive last night. I don't recall ever seeing him so upset."

Stacey's words should have given her hope, but they didn't. Cohen wanted her, but he didn't want to love her. That wasn't enough for her. She wanted to be wanted, to be loved. Was that too much to ask for? Evidently, it was when it came to Cohen Carlson.

Deciding to change the subject, Dee asked, "So, what do you have planned for today?"

"Eden invited us over to help her get ready for the big Memorial Day cookout tomorrow. She makes a big deal of it every year. I hope you don't mind tagging along to help."

Dee smiled. "No, I don't mind, at all. It sounds like fun."

**

"I'm glad you decided to come with me to the folks' house, today," Tyson Steele said as he turned down the road that would take them to his parents' home. "Mom's going to feed you, then she'll put you to work getting all that patio furniture out of storage. Hunter's been here most of the day helping with the decorations. And I'm sure Stacey is here as well."

"I don't mind helping out," Cohen said, fighting to keep his voice from betraying the turmoil going on inside of him. He'd been worked up ever since he'd learned that Dee wouldn't be leaving Phoenix until Tuesday. So if Stacey was here, Dee probably was, too.

GUILTY PLEASURE

When Tyson pulled into his parents' driveway, Cohen wasn't surprised to see all the vehicles already parked there. Since this was Memorial Day weekend, a lot of Tyson's out-of-town relatives had opted to stay in town until Tuesday.

After the basketball game--which the Phoenix Steeles had won--Cohen had gone back to his hotel to shower. Thoughts of Dee had been running through his mind the entire time. Tyson must have thought he would change his mind about going to the party, because he'd volunteered to swing by the hotel and pick him up. So here he was, within moments of seeing Dee again. The thought had his stomach doing summersaults.

"You sure you're okay?"

He glanced over at Tyson, who was bringing the car to a stop. "Yeah, man, I'm fine."

"I know you said what's bothering you is personal, but if you ever want to talk about it, let me know."

He nodded slowly. "I will."

They got out of the vehicle and were instantly overwhelmed by the sound of loud, raucous voices from inside the house. "That's Donovan and Morgan. I guess they're not very good losers," Tyson said, chuckling.

Donovan and Morgan Steele were Tyson's cousins from North Carolina. "Sounds like it," Cohen agreed.

78

The minute they walked into Tyson's parents' home, Cohen saw Dee. To be honest, they saw each other at the same time. And what seemed like a lightning bolt of desire hit him, nearly knocking him off his feet. She looked damn good. Her short, curly hair cut was starting to grow on him. It suited her face. And the shorts and tank top she was wearing definitely suited her figure.

"You okay?"

He broke eye contact with Dee to glance over at Tyson. His best friend was too astute for his own good. Instead of giving Tyson a yes or no answer, he said, "I need a cold beer." He really could have used something stronger, but beer would have to do for now.

Tyson chuckled. "Follow me."

Cohen had been to Tyson's parents' home often enough to know that Tyson was leading him down to the basement. But this was no ordinary basement. It was what Tyson and his brothers liked to refer to as their parents' hideout. There was a huge wall-to-wall cooler packed with all kinds of drinks, including beer and wine, a theater room, a guest bedroom, a dance floor--since the older Steeles enjoyed dancing—a his and hers spa, an exercise room, two huge bathrooms and a kitchenette.

Before they could reach the stairs, they were stopped by a number of people who congratulated them on their win.

"You should feel lucky that we included you on the winning team," Tyson teased Cohen as they continued on their way.

"Whatever."

When they finally reached the basement, Cohen glanced around. He'd always liked the set-up down here.

"Here you are," Tyson said, handing him a beer bottle.

"Thanks." Cohen immediately popped the cap and took a long swig.

"Looks like you needed that."

Cohen just shook his head. "Honestly, I could use something stronger.

"Just from seeing Dee?"

Cohen didn't say anything. It had been more than just seeing her. It had been that strong sexual chemistry that had flowed between them, more than anything. There was no need to share that part with Tyson, but then again, he had a feeling he didn't have to. His friend was overly astute when it pertained to anything sexual. "Yeah, just from seeing Dee."

Tyson leaned against a table. "I felt those vibes, man. Any reason the two of you can't just get it on like normal people?"

"Get it on?"

"Yeah," Tyson said grinning. "I could give you a few pointers, if you need them."

Cohen couldn't help but chuckle as he shook his head. "No thanks."

"Then what's the problem?"

He could deny there wasn't a problem, but he knew Tyson would keep pushing for information. Not because he was nosy, but out of concern.

"It's Dee. At one time, she thought she was in love with me."

Tyson nodded. "And?"

"I can't love her back."

Tyson took a swig of his beer. "Can't love her? Or won't?"

"Does it matter?"

"I think so, Tyson said, staring at him. "There's a difference."

Cohen paused for a minute, then he said, "Okay, I can't."

"Mind if I ask why? She seems like a nice girl."

Cohen frowned. "She *is* a nice girl. That's why she deserves better."

"Better than what?"

"Better than me."

Tyson lifted a brow. "Oh, I don't know. I don't think most women would think you were a bad catch, being a top neurosurgeon and all."

Cohen took another mouthful of beer, trying to figure out what to say. Finally, he admitted, "I can't love her, Tyson. I'm incapable of loving her."

Tyson didn't say anything for a long moment. "I thought I was incapable of loving any woman too, you know. You, of all people, knew how I operated when it came to the opposite sex. Then Hunter came along and changed my mindset real quick. If I can fall in love, so can you."

Cohen stared down at his beer bottle a minute, before looking up at Tyson. "There's a major difference in my situation and yours."

"What's the difference?"

"You've never had your heart broken."

Tyson just looked at him, a questioning expression on his face. "No, I haven't. You have?"

"Yes." Cohen drained his bottle of beer. But he held on to it, his hands gripping it tightly. "Her name was Amanda Forrestal." For the next twenty minutes, Cohen told Tyson about Amanda. It was the first time he'd ever told anyone.

Cohen slammed the beer bottle down on the table. "Damn man, I'd never felt such betrayal in my life. Losing Dad was hard. That, in itself, nearly destroyed me. But I knew I had to be strong for Mom and Stacey. Stace was only ten at the time and had always been a Daddy's girl. Mom put on a brave front, but I knew she wasn't okay.

But returning to school and accepting what Amanda had done almost killed me. I shut myself off from everyone, trying to come to terms, on my own, with how she'd betrayed me, as well as grieve for my dad."

"That was almost eighteen years ago, right?"

"Yes."

"I'd think, after all this time, you would have gotten over some of it by now."

Cohen drew in a deep breath. "There's more." He picked up another bottle of beer—supplied by Tyson, who obviously knew he was going to need it--and took another swig. "I succumbed to a state of depression unlike anything I'd ever experienced."

He then told Tyson how things had been for him, how he'd nearly had a nervous breakdown and how one of his professors had saved him. "The fear of falling back into that black hole still consumes me. Depression nearly destroyed me. I can't take the risk of it ever happening again."

"And you never told anyone, not even your mother or Stacey, what you were going through?" Tyson asked in a low voice.

"No. I didn't want them blaming themselves or seeing me as weak. I needed to be strong for them. They needed my strength, not my weakness."

"What about your aunt?"

"Dad was her brother. The two of them were close. She was going through her own grief."

"Did you ever see Amanda again after college?"

"Yes. I ran into her and husband number two at a fundraiser a few years ago in Boston. I understand her marriage to the senator's son only lasted a couple of years. Her second husband is older, but appears to be rolling in dough. So I guess she's happy."

"Do you still love her?"

"No. But she taught me a very painful lesson, Tyson. One I won't ever forget. That's why I could never love Dee or anyone else. I can't ever allow myself to be emotionally vulnerable again."

Tyson didn't say anything for a minute and then he walked back over to the cooler to grab himself another beer. He popped the top and took a mouthful before returning to Cohen. "You know what I think?"

Cohen had a feeling he wouldn't want to hear what Tyson thought. But he asked anyway. "No, what?"

"I think you're not being fair to Dee. She's not like this Amanda and I believe, deep down, you know that. She wouldn't tell you she loved you if she didn't. Dee wouldn't hurt you that way."

"I didn't say she would. All I'm saying is that I can't take that risk. The thought of falling that hard and becoming vulnerable again scares the shit out of me. Trust me, if there was anyone I wished I could fall in love with, it would be Dee. But I can't." He glanced at his watch. "Come on, let's go back upstairs before Stacey begins wondering where I am."

Tyson nodded. "Okay. Your secret is safe with me."

Cohen nodded. "It was time for me to tell someone. I know it won't go any further. That's what best friends are for, right?"

**

Dee didn't move until she was certain Cohen and Tyson had gone back upstairs to join the others. She hadn't meant to eavesdrop. In fact, she'd already been in the basement when she'd heard their voices. She'd needed to pull herself together after seeing Cohen, and had come downstairs for a little privacy. She'd had no idea Cohen and Tyson would come down, as well, and engage in such deep, emotional conversation. And it had been emotional. At least for Cohen.

Her heart ached for him. How dare that woman betray him like that? It still stunned her, the thought of Cohen in that state. He was a man who was always in control. Cool and calm. She couldn't imagine him slipping into a deep state of depression, the way he'd described. She was grateful for the professor who'd recognized the signs and had found him help.

At least now, she knew why Cohen was keeping her at arm's length. It had nothing to do with their ages or her desirability. He was just trying to protect himself. Amanda hadn't deserved his love.

She began pacing, not only to ease her anger at the woman who'd made things so difficult for her, but also to stall for some time before she went back to the party. The last thing she wanted was for Cohen to notice her coming up the stairs. Then he would know she'd heard his secret, a secret he hadn't shared with anyone, not even Stacey.

Dee recalled when she'd first met Cohen.

She and Stacey had become friends when Stacey had moved in with her Aunt Maggie. Maggie Albright had attended the same church as Dee's parents and she and Stacey had met one Sunday after church. Then school had started a few weeks later and they'd found themselves in a number of the same classes. Over the course of the school year, they'd become the best of friends.

Stacey had always talked about her big brother who was in medical school, and how she couldn't wait for him to get serious about a woman so she could have a sister-in-law. That day had never come. Dee knew that Stacey believed it was because Cohen gave everything to his career. But all this time, he'd been only protecting himself.

She couldn't claim to imagine what he was going through and couldn't ever recall getting truly depressed about anything. Even when Cohen had rejected her that first time, she'd been willing to wait it out and hope he'd change his mind. The second time, she'd been hurt and discouraged, but she'd managed to move on.

All she had to do was recall the sound of his voice while he'd been talking to Tyson. It had been raw, gut-wrenching. She could actually feel the pain he still harbored in his heart, the pain that still consumed him.

Dee fought back the tears that threatened to fall. He could offer a lot to a woman, if he'd only allow himself to do so, but he wouldn't. Then, she remembered something else he'd said. "*...if there was anyone I wished I could fall in love with, it would be Dee...*"

Should those words give her hope or was he a lost cause? Did she owe it to herself to discover which one it was? What if, in the end, she was the one left with a broken heart? His two rejections had hurt. Could she risk him loving him a third time?

"Okay," she said to herself as she stopped pacing. "Is he worth it?" She knew the answer without thinking about it. Yes, he was worth it.

She'd taken Psychology in college and knew how serious depression could be. She could understand why he'd try so hard to protect himself from any future lapses. How could she prove to him that she wouldn't hurt him, if only he'd trust her with his heart?

Drawing in a deep breath, she frowned in deep thought. The first thing she had to do was convince him that she was different from this Amanda. He'd told Tyson that she was different, but did he really believe that? He also thought he could never return her love. Could she find a way to prove him wrong?

She tapped a finger to her chin, thinking.

And according to her brothers, a thinking Dee was a dangerous one.

7

"Okay, what do you have to tell me?"

Dee glanced across the breakfast table at Stacey. Eli had just left to go to his parents' home to help his father start grilling the meat. According to Stacey, the elder Steeles had invited a lot of people to their Memorial Day cookout this year.

Dee placed her fork down. She'd decided to tell Stacey what she'd overheard, though not all of it. The part about Cohen's bout with depression was something Stacey needed to hear directly from Cohen. Hopefully, one day he would share that part of his life with his sister.

Yesterday when Dee had finally left the basement, she'd been relieved to find Cohen and Tyson nowhere in sight. Most of the men had gathered outside to help Drew set up tables and chairs on the patio.

"I think I know the reason Cohen keeps rejecting me."

Stacey placed her coffee cup down. "What is it?"

Before answering, Dee decided to ask a question of her own. "Did you know that Cohen was in love before? And that the woman broke his heart?"

Stacey lifted her brows. "Cohen? In love? Where did you hear that from?"

"Cohen."

"He told you that?"

Dee shook her head. "No, I overheard him talking to Tyson." Dee then elaborated on the conversation in the basement.

"Let me get this straight," Stacey said, leaning in closer. "Cohen was in love? But when Dad died, the woman dumped him?"

"Yes. He'd cared for her a lot. I could hear it in his voice when he was talking to Tyson. She definitely left a wound he refuses to let heal."

Stacey shook her head slowly. "I should have been more perceptive where Cohen was concerned," Stacey said sadly. "I should have guessed there was more to his reluctance to change his bachelor status."

"And how could you have known when he didn't tell you?" Dee asked her, refusing to let her friend play the blame game.

"I should have suspected something, especially when he didn't take the bait with Linda Miller."

Dee cocked a brow. "Linda Miller? Music teacher Linda Miller?"

"Yes. It was that summer that you spent with your grandparents in Kentucky. Aunt Maggie made me continue my piano lessons all summer. Cohen helped out by picking me up from Linda's a few times."

Dee remembered Linda Miller well. She'd been eight years older than her and Stacey. She was a music teacher in one of the schools and also taught private piano lessons in her home.

"And?"

"And I suspected she liked Cohen because on those days she knew Cohen would be picking me up, she'd dress up a bit and flirt with him."

"And you tried to get them together?" Dee angrily accused.

"Yes."

"How could you do that when you knew I loved him?"

Stacey rolled her eyes. "Get real, Dee. We were only fifteen."

"Doesn't matter."

Stacey shook her head. "You hadn't told me you loved Cohen, at that point, remember?"

No, she hadn't. "Okay, so what happened?"

Stacey leaned back comfortably in her chair and took another sip of coffee. "When I noticed how interested Linda was in Cohen, all I could think about was that she would make a great big sister-in-law. So I put a plan into motion."

"What did you do?"

"I told Cohen to pick me up at Linda's, and then I cancelled the lesson, knowing she would invite him to stay for dinner."

"Did he stay?"

"No. But from what I gather, she didn't let on that I wasn't there until after she'd let him in. But whatever she did really upset him. Cohen never gave me specifics, but something happened to make him really angry—at her and at me. He figured out I'd set him up and didn't like it. I apologized and he made me promise never to interfere in his love life again. And to this day, I haven't." She paused, and took another sip of coffee. "I often wondered why he wasn't interested in Linda. I thought she was gorgeous," Stacey said.

Dee shrugged. "She looked alright."

"Stop being petty. She looked better than alright and you know it."

"Whatever." Yes, she knew it. At the time, she and Stacey had thought Linda Miller was everything they'd wanted to be when they grew up. She was beautiful, sophisticated, educated and confidant. She turned men's heads wherever she went. Dee shouldn't be so happy that Linda couldn't hold Cohen's interest, but she was.

"So what do you think happened?" Dee asked, hoping Stacey might know something she didn't.

"I can only assume Linda came on too strong and he didn't like it."

Dee didn't say anything. She'd thought he'd liked it when she'd come on strong. Funny.

She'd spent most of the night trying to figure out what she was going to do about Cohen. She had to have a plan, something well thought out, something foolproof. And once she knew what she was going to do, she'd make sure she kept it to herself. She didn't want Stacey to have to break her promise to her brother.

Beth, Lawyer's fiancée, had told her that Cohen had already sent in his RSVP to attend their June wedding. And according to Stacey, he planned to stay an additional few days in Memphis to handle business with the property manager looking after his aunt Maggie's home. By then,

Dee hoped to have a solid idea of what she was going to do. After overhearing Cohen's conversation with Tyson, she knew she had to do something. For so long, he had shut himself off, not sharing his pain and misery with anyone, even after all these years. There could be no healing until he faced his past. She believed that and needed to help him believe it, as well. That's why she needed to be careful. The thought of not succeeding a third time left her stomach in knots. This time, the stakes were too high. She couldn't fail.

"Well, at least you know it's not you, Dee," Stacey said, breaking into her thoughts. "My heart goes out to him and I hope that one day he can get past it. I felt the same way after I broke up with Wallace. I hadn't thought I'd ever get seriously involved again. Then Eli came along."

"And?" Dee knew the story but wanted to hear Stacey say it anyway. She wanted to be sure that whatever steps she took to win Cohen's love would be the right ones.

"And Eli was too darn irresistible. I just couldn't help myself."

Too darn irresistible... Umm, Dee thought. Unknowingly, Stacey had planted a seed in her head. One thing she knew about Cohen was that he had an ingrained sense of responsibility to look after those he cared deeply about. If he thought she was making a bad decision, he'd have no choice but to reveal those protective instincts.

What if…

An idea popped into her head. It would be risky, but given Cohen's propensity to shield those he cared about from harm, it just might work.

She would see him at the cookout today. And when she did, she intended to test the waters. If he reacted the way she hoped he would, she'd waste no time putting the rest of her plan into action.

**

As far as Cohen was concerned, nobody could throw a party like the Steeles. When he'd lived in Phoenix, he'd been invited to a number of get-togethers and he always had a good time. He knew the majority of the people who'd come, though not all. But there was one guy, in particular, that he wished hadn't showed up. His gaze had latched onto Midas Coronado the moment he arrived. The man had immediately started searching the crowd, no doubt looking for Dee.

Cohen would have probably liked Midas under normal circumstances, but for some reason, the guy's interest in Dee bothered him. It shouldn't, but it did. Mainly because he knew what type of man Midas was. The fact that he'd joined the Guarded Hearts Club spoke volumes.

Cohen was about to go outside and join Tyson and the others outside on the patio when the front door opened and Eli, Stacey and Dee walked in. Dee glanced around the room, seeming not to even notice him before her gaze lit on Midas. She smiled brightly at the man. Cohen watched Midas smile back before walking over to her.

The deep pang of jealousy he felt at that moment nearly toppled him over. It didn't help that Dee was wearing a denim miniskirt that showed too much thigh and a pair of stilettos that emphasized her gorgeous legs. She looked hot…and it was killing him.

"Well, hello, my handsome brother."

He turned to look down at his sister. He hadn't realized Eli and Stacey had crossed the room to see him.

He drew Stacey into his arms for a hug. "Hey sis." He then gave Eli a fist bump. "Hey man. You two okay?"

Eli smiled broadly. "I doubt we could be any better, or happier." He glanced down at his wife. "I can't imagine a time when she wasn't in my life."

Cohen believed him. "I'm happy for you both. Do you care whether the upcoming arrival is a boy or a girl?"

Stacey chuckled. "I'd like a daughter, but I think Eli is worried she might date someone like him."

Eli tightened his arms around his wife's waist and smiled down at her. "That's true." Then he glanced up at Cohen. "So when are you going to check out of the hotel and spend some time at our place?" he asked.

Cohen smiled, trying not to notice Dee and Midas out of the corner of his eye. "I like the hotel just fine, thanks. Besides, you already have a houseguest."

"Doesn't matter. We have plenty of room. Besides, Dee is leaving tomorrow. She's heading out for Virginia Beach."

Cohen lifted a brow. "Virginia Beach?"

"Yes." Eli glanced around. "We better go find the folks to let them know we're here."

"I'll go with you," Cohen said. It was either go with them or remain inside and continue giving Midas and Dee dirty looks.

"You okay?" Stacey asked him, looping their arms as they walked outside.

He smiled down at his sister. "Yeah, I'm fine." At the moment, he wished that was true.

Outside, Tyson was helping his father man the grill, while Eden was being the perfect hostess. Her green eyes lit up when she saw Eli and Stacey. Cohen knew she was excited about getting another grandchild.

He was just about to say something to Stacey when he noticed Dee and Midas. They'd come outside on the patio as well. The man had his arms around her waist, the palm of his hand resting entirely too close to Dee's ass. Cohen's own hand tightened on his beer so hard, it was a wonder the bottle didn't shatter. What the hell was she thinking, letting Coronado touch her so inappropriately?

"You okay, man?"

He turned towards Eli. His brother in-law was looking at him oddly. "Yes. Why wouldn't I be?"

Eli smiled. "You just growled."

Had he? He glanced at Stacey, and her concerned smile told him that he had, indeed, made such a sound. He chugged down the last of his beer and glanced back over at Dee. Now she had two other guys practically hanging on to her every word. And Midas's hand was still too close to her ass to suit Cohen.

Suddenly, unexplainably, he saw red. "Excuse me," he said to Eli and Stacey. Before he could stop himself, he strode across the patio to where Dee stood with her admirers.

As if she sensed his approach, she looked up. Their gazes connected and held. He fought back the urge to glare at the three men. Instead, he ignored them, not so much as acknowledging their presence. His attention was focused solely on Dee.

"Hi Cohen," she said, her features unreadable. "What's going on?"

"I need to talk to you for a second, Dee."

At that moment, he wasn't sure she'd agree. But he knew that the last thing she'd want would be for him to make a scene. *Make a scene*? When had that even become a possibility for him?

She didn't say anything at first. Finally, she nodded. "Excuse me for a minute," she said to her admirers, before turning back to him. "Okay, Cohen. Lead the way."

**

Dee tried to keep up with Cohen as he led her back inside the house. When he moved toward the stairs to the basement, she knew they were going to the place where she'd discovered his secrets only yesterday.

Honestly, Dee hadn't expected him to take the bait so soon. She figured she'd need to flirt a bit more with Midas and a few of the other single men before she got a rise out of him. She had deliberately ignored Cohen since she'd arrived, and had let Midas touch her in a way she normally wouldn't have done. When he'd outrageously flirted with her, she'd flirted back, knowing Cohen was looking. And Cohen was pissed. She could see it in the way he was clenching and unclenching his hands, almost as if he wanted to ring someone's neck. Probably hers.

Whether he realized it or not, the fact that he was upset meant something. At least, it did to her. Cohen was not a man who displayed a lot of emotion. Somehow, he always managed to keep himself in check. But in order for her to succeed, she had to rattle him, make him lose control.

He moved aside to let her precede him down the stairs, then he followed. He looked around to make sure they were alone, something he hadn't done yesterday when he'd spoken with Tyson. Those gorgeous brown eyes glared at her.

"Okay, Cohen. What do we need to talk about?"

"What is going on with you, Dee?" he asked in a harsh tone.

She feigned ignorance. "I have no idea what you mean?"

"You were letting Coronado paw you in public," he snapped.

"So what? Why do you care?" she snapped back.

Her question seemed to throw him for a loop. Then he said, "Because it doesn't look good."

She rolled her eyes. "I don't see anyone but you getting all worked up about it. Maybe it's because I'm an adult--a single woman who's drawn to a single man."

"Drawn to him? Are you telling me there's something going on between the two of you? Are you sleeping together?"

She hadn't expected *that* question, at least, not yet. "I don't believe that's any of your business. You've made it clear that you didn't want me. What does it matter to you if someone else does?"

"Midas Coronado isn't good for you, Dee. He's a player. There's no way he can make you happy."

Dee glared back at him. "You could have said the same thing about Eli, yet Stacey seems happy enough, doesn't she?"

He stared down at the floor for a minute, then lifted his face to stare back at her, a knowing look in his eyes. "Is that what this is all about? All this attention seeking from Midas?"

"What is it to you?"

"Don't do it, Dee. You are better than that."

She took a step forward, getting in his face. "Am I? Am I better than anyone but you, Cohen? If that's the case, why did you reject me?" When he didn't say anything, she continued. "Twice, you've told me that I meant nothing to you and--"

"I never said you meant nothing to me. You do. You're Stacey's--"

"Please don't tell me that all I am to you is your sister's best friend. You've said it enough. I get it. It hurt at the time, but I've moved on. I'm over you, Cohen. In fact, thanks to you, I don't intend to fall in love. It's not worth it. But you wouldn't know anything about that, loving someone and being rejected, hurting so much that you'd do anything to avoid feeling the pain again. Well, that's what I'm doing, Cohen. Protecting my heart. From now on, I'm going to do what I want, when I want, with who I want." *There.* She hoped her words hit a nerve and gave him something to think about.

"What do you mean?"

"I mean that there will be no happily-ever-after in my future, so I might as well do things a little differently. I plan to enjoy my life--get buck wild, so to speak--and not worry about falling in love. Because for me, it won't happen again. So why not have some fun with guys who feel the same way? If that labels me an attention-seeker, then so be it. I have the next two weeks to seek all the attention I want in Virginia Beach. And you better believe I'm ready."

Standing this close to him, she was tempted to use the tip of her tongue to lick his lips, from corner to corner. She wanted to do it. Honestly, she did. Knowing such a thing would screw up her plans, though, she dropped her hands to her side and stepped back from temptation. "Being with you introduced me to needs I hadn't realized I had, Cohen, sexual needs that my toy boyfriend can't handle. No toy will ever compare to you."

The shocked look that suddenly appeared on his face told her she'd probably said too much, but she needed to paint a believable picture for him. "Don't worry about me, Cohen. You've made it clear I have no place in your life. I am not your responsibility."

She paused a minute, then drew in a deep breath and sealed the deal. "I'm flying out in the morning. I hope you have a nice flight back to Florida."

With a haughty toss of her head, she turned around and walked back up the stairs. It was done.

**

Cohen couldn't move. Her words had stopped him cold. And watching her long legs in stilettos sashay up the stairs in that sexy miniskirt overloaded his senses. Her outfit was so short that a glimpse of her blue panties flashed him as she climbed the steps.

He drew in a long, labored breath, going through the conversation in his mind again, just to make sure he hadn't imagined it. She was going to Virginia Beach for two weeks to have fun? And her definition of fun was to get buck wild?

Jeez. He rubbed his hand down his face. He couldn't believe she'd actually said those things to him. But a part of him was glad he knew of her plans, so he could stop her from ruining her life. He wondered if she'd said anything to Stacey. Then again, if she had, wouldn't Stacey have tried to talk her out of it?

He quickly moved up the stairs and walked back out to the patio. He glanced around, looking for his sister. He saw that Dee was back with Midas. Forcing himself to ignore that fact, he continued his search, finally locating Stacey and Eli. They were talking to Tyson and Hunter. He swiftly moved in their direction.

"Stacey, can I speak with you privately for a moment?" he asked, taking hold of his sister's hand, as if he intended to talk to her, regardless.

She lifted concerned eyes to his. "Sure." Then she turned to the others. "I'll be back in a minute."

Cohen pulled her to a quiet spot beneath a huge tree, away from the others, but close enough that he could keep an inconspicuous eye on Dee.

"Cohen? What is it?"

"It's Dee. "Do you know of her plans?"

Stacey lifted a brow. "What plans?"

"Where she intends to go when she leaves here tomorrow, and what she plans to do."

From his sister's expression, he knew she was having a hard time following his train of thought. "Dee told me she's going to spend two weeks in Virginia Beach. As for her plans, I assume she'd going to kick off her summer with rest and relaxation."

"Wrong."

"Wrong? What are you talking about?"

"I just talked to her. She plans to make herself available...to any man looking for some fun."

Stacey didn't say anything, as if she was expecting him to say more. "And?"

He frowned. "Isn't that enough?"

Stacey shook her head. "No. She plans to meet someone and enjoy herself. What's wrong with that?"

"It's how she plans to enjoy herself. That's what we should be worried about."

"And do you know how she plans to enjoy herself, Cohen?"

"She plans to sleep around."

Stacey didn't say anything for a minute, then asked, "And she told you that?"

"Yes, she pretty much insinuated as much."

Stacey shrugged her shoulders. "Dee is twenty-seven-years old, definitely old enough to do what she wants."

Cohen stared at his sister in disbelief. "Is that all you've got to say?"

"I don't know what you want from me, Cohen. Dee is smart and intelligent. I'm sure she'll practice safe sex and--"

"I would think, as her best friend, you'd try to talk her out of doing something as crazy as that."

"Why? Single men go on vacation and hook up with women all the time."

"That's beside the point."

"Then tell me, what is the point, Cohen? You're acting like a jealous lover again. Dee is a grown woman. If she plans to have a swinging good time for two weeks on vacation, who is she hurting?"

"She could end up hurting herself. I don't like it."

"Well, as Dee's best friend, I want her to be happy. At least she's not pining for you anymore, since you let her know you weren't interested."

"I have my reasons."

"Do you? What are they?"

He didn't say anything. The last thing he wanted was to talk about Amanda. One day, he would tell her sister everything. But not now. "I'm not interested in the type of relationship she wants."

"Well, she evidently heard you, loud and clear, Cohen. You hurt her."

"I didn't ask her to fall in love with me," he said, annoyance creeping into his voice.

"No, you didn't. But she did. Luckily, she's finally come to terms with the fact that you won't return that love. So she's doing what it takes to get over you. I figure, whatever she plans to do in Virginia Beach is her way of moving on."

"She's making a huge mistake. Somebody needs to be looking out for her. Keeping her in check."

"Well, it won't be me. We all experience disappointment and heartbreak in different ways. Some people go into their shell and don't ever come out, not willing to risk their hearts again. Others decide to get over it by jumping in and taking whatever life has to offer. Dee has figured out how she wants to handle this, Cohen. I suggest you accept it." She turned at the sound of laughter coming from the patio. "Now unless there's something else, I plan to get back to the party."

"Fine."

Stacey walked off, but he remained where he was, watching Dee. She looked like a beautiful angel and a naughty sex kitten, all rolled into one. What she was going through was all his fault. He should never have touched her.

She'd said he'd hurt her, but he couldn't see the sense in apologizing for telling her the truth about his feelings. For trying to spare her from wasting her love on him. Still, the last thing he'd wanted to do was throw her out there to the wolves.

A short while later, he knew what he had to do. Someone needed to look out for her. If the job fell on him, then so be it. Luckily, he had some time off from the hospital. It had been years since he'd been to Virginia Beach. Now looked like a great time for another visit.

**

A knock on the door made Dee glance up from folding her laundry. "Come in."

Stacey smiled as she entered the room. "I came to see how your packing is going."

"Not much to it. I only used a few things. Thanks for letting me use your washer and dryer."

"No problem," Stacey said, sitting on the edge of the bed. "Just so you know...I think you rattled Cohen today. But then, that was your plan, wasn't it?"

Dee stopped packing and glanced over at Stacey. "It really wasn't a plan. Let's just say, I was testing the waters on a theory I had. I didn't want to tell you anything. That way, Cohen couldn't accuse you of interfering in his love life."

Stacey shook her head, chuckling. "If I'm interfering, it's because of Cohen. He's worried about you. Evidently you shared a different version of your plans for Virginia Beach with him than you did with me," she said, giving her a pointed look.

Dee rolled her eyes. "I just wanted to make him mad."

"Well, I think you did more than that. I think you drove him crazy."

Dee lifted her chin. "Serves him right."

"You might be right, but you may have gone overboard. Evidently, he thinks you needs a babysitter in Virginia Beach. He's contemplating doing the honors."

Dee blinked. "You're kidding, right?"

Stacy smiled and shook her head. "No, I'm not kidding. Cohen called a few moments ago. He said he's leaving Phoenix earlier than he'd planned. I figured he was returning to Florida. But when I mentioned it to Eli, he wasn't surprised. He said Cohen had asked him where you would be staying in Virginia Beach. I'm pretty sure he intends to follow you there to make sure you stay out of trouble."

A huge smile touched Dee's lips. "Truthfully? He believes he has to do that?"

Stacey chuckled again. "Evidently. After you told him of your plans, he had a major conniption. Now he's convinced he has to save you from yourself."

Dee threw her head back and laughed. "That's wonderful."

"Wonderful? Having Cohen follow you to Virginia Beach doesn't bother you?" Stacey asked.

"No." Dee began pacing the room. Then she stopped and looked at Stacey. "I need to prove to Cohen that he can trust me with his heart. That he doesn't have to be afraid to fall in love again."

She drew in a deep breath. "I had planned to use my time in Virginia Beach to come up with a plan, something I could put into play when I saw him at Lawyer's wedding. But now, I've got the perfect opportunity to act sooner. And whether he realizes it or not, he's given me an idea."

"He has?"

"Yes. Twice, I've seduced your brother, only for him to retreat. This time, he'll be the one to seduce me."

Stacey gave her a dubious look. "Honestly? Do you think you'll be able to pull that off?"

Dee nodded. "I certainly intend to try. While in Virginia Beach, I'm going to drive Cohen so crazy with lust, he'll have to give in. And I'll be waiting for him when it happens."

8

Cohen unpacked the last of his things and placed them in the dresser drawers. He usually lived out of his luggage while traveling, since he was never in the same place for long. However, this time around, he would be spending at least a week, possibly two--whatever length of time it took to make sure Dee didn't carry out this crazy plan of hers.

He couldn't get the image of her out of his mind, how she'd stood directly in front of him that day in the basement, with her arms crossed under her breasts, glaring at him. It had been blatantly clear she'd been upset, just like it had been damn obvious she hadn't been wearing a bra. It had been hard to concentrate on her face without letting his gaze dip to her chest. She'd been so intent on giving him a piece of her mind that she hadn't noticed his preoccupation with her chest. At least, until she'd start talking about coming here to seek out male attention.

It hadn't been hard to find out where she'd be staying. He had known better than to ask Stacey, but he'd figured

Eli would know. His brother-in-law hadn't disappointed him, providing him with the name of the resort and the dates Dee would be staying. That was all Cohen had needed to book a room for himself.

Now here he was, ensconced at the Turtle Dove Resort. Walking over to the window, he took a good look around the place. It was a vacationer's paradise. All the rooms had an ocean view and he'd been given a brochure listing all the daily activities.

This place was a singles' resort. He hadn't been surprised. After all, there had to be single men available if Dee intended to carry out her plans. She'd arrived one day before him and he hoped she hadn't found any trouble yet.

Cohen reassured himself once again that he was doing the right thing. Whether she'd intended to or not, the other night, she'd told him he was basically responsible for making her come here. If he hadn't slept with her, she wouldn't be looking for someone else to give her mind-blowing orgasms. She'd been a virgin, for God's sake!

But the big question was...how was he going to stop her from getting naughty with some other guy? Whatever it took, he planned to do it.

He picked up the brochure. There would be a welcome party tonight on the beach. She'd undoubtedly be there, which meant he would be too. Cohen smiled, thinking of her reaction when she saw him. He couldn't wait to see it. He pushed aside the thought that he couldn't wait to see her, either.

*

Dee drew in a deep breath as she hung up the phone. Cohen had arrived. All she'd had to do was call the check-in desk and give his name. They'd acknowledged his arrival but wouldn't pass along his room number. She didn't need it. If he was here to keep an eye on her, she knew she'd find him before long. And when she did, she would feign surprise and then outrage that he'd followed her. Then, of course, she would pretend to ignore him…even though she knew he probably wouldn't let her.

She had a pretty good idea that he'd be at the welcome party tonight. And when their paths crossed, she'd be ready. She would show him that he couldn't just show up at the resort—a singles' resort—and expect to keep things platonic. He had a lot to learn about women if he assumed that.

She glanced at her watch and then down at herself. Tonight's affair was being held in the resort's ballroom and the attire was dressy. She decided to wear her red cocktail party dress with a draped V-back. She had bought it last year while visiting her aunt Rhonda in Atlanta. What she liked most about the dress was how good it looked with her red stilettos.

Glancing in the mirror, she smiled at her reflection. The short, curly hair style was growing on her, and when Cohen had admitted that he liked it, it had boosted her self-confidence and given her renewed hope. Her goal was to get him to see her as someone other than Stacey's best friend. She wanted him to see her as the woman he wanted.

Drawing in a deep breath for courage, she grabbed her small purse off the table, then headed for the door.

**

Cohen walked toward the ballroom, shaking his head. He'd just turned down an offer from a woman who'd been bold enough to invite him up to her hotel room for what she claimed would be a night he wouldn't forget. He frowned as he grabbed a drink off the tray of a passing waiter. He hoped Dee wasn't crazy enough to do something like that.

The thought that she just might bothered him so much that he emptied the contents of his wine glass in a single gulp. He was licking his lips when a sudden feeling of heat raced up his spine. He didn't have to see her to know that Dee had entered the room.

He turned to look at the entrance of the ballroom, and there she stood. And he wasn't the only man looking. Tonight she was the lady in red. Scorching hot. Desire in flames. There was something about the way she looked that had him wanting another drink, this one a little stronger.

He wasn't surprised that she'd dressed in such an eye-catching outfit. Simply put, she looked gorgeous. If she'd intended to make her presence at the resort known, she'd succeeded. Cohen hung back for now. She wouldn't be happy to see him. She'd resent him interfering in her life, and would think he didn't have the right. He probably didn't. But he refused to stand by and let her make a huge mistake, just because he'd awakened her desires. Desires she wanted to feel again, but with someone else.

And that was the one thing he didn't want to think about--Dee sharing her body with someone else for all the wrong reasons. Sure, he'd thought she'd slept with him for the wrong reasons, too.

To make sure she didn't see him, he was about to move toward the bar in the back of the room when a conversation between two men standing close by met his ears.

"Will you look at that hot piece in red who just walked in, Marshall."

"I'm looking...and I'm planning to have her in my bed tonight, if not sooner."

Cohen saw red and it took all his control not to let the men know that the only bed Dee would be in tonight was her own. Instead he moved away, though he planned to keep an eye on the guy who'd made such a bold prediction.

"What would you like, sir?"

"Scotch on the rocks."

Cohen glanced over his shoulder and noticed that Dee had already attracted a crowd. Still, he decided to wait it out. He frowned when he saw the guy who'd claimed he'd have Dee in his bed make his move.

Moments later, a drink in hand, he moved to an empty table in the back where he was certain Dee couldn't see him. He sank down in the chair, thinking that this was a good spot to sit and watch. He had to believe that Dee had more sense than to willingly play this game of seduction. But then, he remembered what she'd told him about her plans for these two weeks. Uncertainty gripped his insides.

"Would you like another drink, sir?"

He glanced up at the waiter working the floor and then down at the glass in his hand. He'd finished it off already? "Yes. Another scotch on ice."

GUILTY PLEASURE

Somewhere between Cohen's second and third glasses of scotch, he'd realized he was deeply annoyed. He had seen Tyson in action too many times not to recognize a seduction ploy when he saw one. There was no doubt in his mind that the overconfident jerk was doing his best to seduce Dee, just as he'd bragged earlier. He hadn't left her side all night. They were sharing the same table and had danced a few times. Whatever conversation they were having was evidently entertaining, if Dee's smiles and occasional laughter were anything to go by.

Cohen had been keeping tabs on how many drinks Dee had consumed and was satisfied there hadn't been too many. He'd noticed that whenever the man had summoned the waiter for a refill, she'd had the good sense to refuse.

He saw the man check his watch. Cohen checked his. He glanced back up and saw Dee also checking hers. It was getting late, close to midnight. Dee leaned close and whispered something to the man. Was she inviting him to her room? Was she agreeing to go to his?

He felt a deep punch in his chest when they stood and the man escorted Dee out of the ballroom.

**

Where was Cohen? Dee checked her watch again. She'd been at the party for at least three hours and she'd

118

expected him to make an appearance hours ago. She was hoping that he would, especially since the man walking beside her, Marshall Whitmire, was driving her nuts with his chatter about her joining him in his room.

Of course, she had no intention of doing that, regardless of how good looking he was. He had an ego the size of Texas. Though he'd spent the last hour doing his best to convince her to share his bed tonight, the rest of the night, all he'd done was talk about himself. He was an attorney from Huntsville, Alabama and according to him, his family was as well-known, and had just about as much money as, Bill Gates.

From his attitude, she gathered it was a foregone conclusion on his part that when they left the ballroom, they would be headed up to his room. Although she was disappointed that Cohen hadn't shown up, she had no intention of going anywhere with Marshall. He'd asked her four times already and she'd turned him down every time.

Her thoughts shifted back to Cohen. The hotel staffer had verified he'd checked in. Was she wrong to assume he had come here because of her? "What's your room number, Deidre?"

Marshall's question cut into her thoughts. Obviously, he figured that she'd prefer to have home field advantage. Little did he guess that she had no intention of giving him her room number, or anything else. When they came to the bank of elevators, she stopped, grateful there were a number of people around, in case he refused to take no for an answer. "You don't have to see me to my room, Marshall. I know the way."

A smooth smile touched the corners of his lips. "I didn't intend to see you to your room. Since you won't join me in my room, I thought I'd come to yours."

Like hell you will. She stared at him, seeing the smooth smile become an arrogant grin. She'd encountered egotistical men before, but he had to be one of the pushiest. She was about to put Marshall Whitmire in his place once and for all when a familiar voice stopped her.

"Dee!"

She could tell by Cohen's tone that he wasn't too happy. In fact, it was obvious from his features that he was downright furious. She fought back a sigh of relief, though she knew that, for the moment, she had to pretend to be both surprised and angry at seeing him.

"Hey, I thought you told me your name was Deidre," Marshall said accusingly.

She glanced up at him. "It is. My friends call me Dee." She hoped he grasped the implication. She didn't want him as a friend.

"That guy coming toward us doesn't look happy," Marshall said. "Is he an ex-boyfriend or something?"

"No, he's just a friend," Dee said, returning her gaze to Cohen as he walked toward them.

"And you sure?" Marshall asked

"Depends."

By the time Cohen reached them, Dee had a scowl on her face. "Cohen? What on earth are you doing here?"

"Never mind what I'm doing here. Where are you going with him?"

Marshall obviously had a death wish. "Not that it's any of your business, but we were about to have a nightcap in my room."

Wrong answer, Dee thought when Cohen moved towards Marshall, his fist clenched. She quickly grabbed hold of Cohen's hand. "Don't you dare!" Although she was tempted to, she wasn't about to deny Marshall's lie. Let Cohen think what he wanted. "Cohen, I asked what you're doing here."

"Keeping you from making a big mistake."

Several people had turned to stare at them. Dee quickly figured out a way to diffuse the situation. It would get rid of Marshall and further her strategy with Cohen. She turned to Marshall. "I need to handle this situation. It's personal."

"If he's threatening you, I can call security," Marshall said, glaring at Cohen.

"No," Dee quickly said, placing a hand on Cohen's arm. She snatched it back when a tingling sensation swept through her.

"He doesn't scare me," Marshall argued, missing the sexual tension quickly forming between her and Cohen.

He should scare you, Dee thought. She wondered if Marshall had noticed that Cohen was a lot taller than he was…and much more muscular. Heck, Cohen had even been on the boxing team while at Harvard. "I've got this," she said to Marshall, glad she was finally getting rid of him.

"Will we hook up later?"

Before she could answer, Cohen said, "Hell no!"

She gave Marshall a small smile. "It was nice meeting you, Marshall." Then she turned to Cohen, giving him what she hoped was her meanest glare. "We need to talk. Now!"

It was time to put this plan into action. And she was going to start with the shock effect. She didn't want Cohen to only view her as his kid sister's best friend. She needed him to see her as a woman, with needs like anyone else. A woman who didn't have a problem telling him exactly what she wanted.

Without waiting for him to say anything, she walked off toward the resort's botanical garden.

9

"Stay away from her," Cohen growled between gritted teeth at the man Dee called Marshall. Then, without waiting for a response, he turned and quickly moved toward the direction Dee had gone.

He could see her up ahead and tried not to react to the graceful sway of her hips when she walked. And that ass was what erotic dreams were made of.

Fire licked along his nerve endings with every step she took on those stilettoed heels. And the back of that way-too-sexy red dress left too much skin showing. Skin he remembered touching and tasting.

Slowing his pace, he rubbed his hand down his face. Damn. Why couldn't he control himself where she was concerned? This wasn't just any woman he was checking out. This was Dee, who he'd known forever. Then again, this was also the Dee he'd had in his bed. He knew first-hand how it felt to be between those gorgeous legs, to grip those curvy hips and to find heaven in the depth of her delicious mouth.

When she opened a set of French doors and disappeared, he sighed with relief. But out of sight wasn't out of mind. The moment he stepped out on the terrace that led to the botanical gardens, she was waiting, ready to give him hell. "What do you think you're doing here, Cohen?"

He refused to answer until she'd answered a question for him. "You were going to his hotel room, weren't you?"

She glared at him and crossed her arms over her chest. He wished she hadn't done that. It made her breasts push up and he could clearly see a very nice, tempting cleavage. "And what is it to you if I was?"

A muscle in the back of his neck felt tight, like it was about to pop. "It would have been a mistake."

"Then it would have been my mistake to make. What I do is none of your business. You have no right to be here."

He shoved his hands into the pockets of his pants. "Last I looked, this was a free country."

She rolled her eyes. "Think about what you're doing, Cohen. You followed a woman you don't want, to a place where people are hooking up all over, just to keep her from having some fun with someone else. Why?"

He could definitely answer that. But first he needed to straighten out a few things. "I do want you, Dee. Don't ever think I don't. But it would not be fair of me to have you."

She narrowed her gaze at him. "But you did have me."

"I know. I wish you wouldn't keep reminding me."

He saw anger flare in her eyes. "Why? I know I was inexperienced. Are you insinuating I was *that* bad?"

There was no way he could allow her to think that. "No, you were *that* good." He hadn't meant to say that. Too late.

"Then why Cohen? And please don't tell me it's because I'm Stacey's best friend or that there's an age thing between us."

He shook his head. It was time for the truth. He couldn't use those excuses any longer. "No, none of those."

"Then why?"

He drew in a deep breath. Maybe he ought to come right out and tell her the reason. Tell her about Amanda, about the heartache she'd caused him...about his fear of falling into the abyss of depression again. But what would that accomplish? Knowing Dee like he did, she would take it upon herself to prove he could love again. But he knew he couldn't. His heart was no longer broken. It was hardened. There was a difference. He was incapable of loving anyone and he knew it.

When he didn't say anything, she poked his chest. "This doesn't make sense. You don't want to sleep with me, but you don't want anyone else to, either. You can't have it both ways. You have no idea what I'm going through, Cohen. How it's been since you first touched me."

Cohen knew he shouldn't ask, but he couldn't help himself. "And what are you going through, Dee?"

"Where should I start? With my need to have a man's hands on me, a man's body moving inside me. Or those erotic dreams I have of you tasting every inch of me?"

Jeez. Why did she have to go there and remind him of how it had been? He could feel his erection get hard, just remembering. "I think that's too much information."

"Then you shouldn't have asked. I don't appreciate you trying to throw a monkey wrench into my sex life, when yours is probably just fine and dandy."

If only she knew, he thought. Still, there was no need to tell her that he hadn't been with another woman since their last night together. At first, he'd convinced himself it was because he'd felt guilty about what they'd done. About the fact that he couldn't give her what she needed.

"I'm not here because of me, Dee."

She took a step closer. "And you shouldn't be here because of me. I'm twenty-seven. An adult. Living on my own. And I'm in my right mind."

"Your actions tonight tell me otherwise, Dee. You were about to sleep with a stranger."

She rolled his eyes. "Trust me. I wasn't seriously interested in Marshall, not for anything long term. But for tonight, I knew all I needed to know about him…that he could get hard and he wanted me."

There was no way Cohen could hide his shock. Then she twisted the blade a little deeper. "He's going to need a pretty stiff erection to satisfy me, not to mention stamina. I was looking forward to tonight, Cohen. And you ruined it for me."

He could only stare at her while standing there doing the very thing she'd assured herself good old Marshall could do. Get hard. Because she was standing so close, not to mention glaring at him, she probably hadn't noticed his predicament. But if she got any closer, his erection would poke her. "Dammit Dee, you shouldn't say things like that."

She waved off his words. "Whatever. If you weren't here, you wouldn't have to concern yourself about me. What I do is my business."

She was right. If she wanted to sleep with that guy, there wasn't a damn thing he could do about it. "Can we talk about this?"

She rolled her eyes at him. "Honestly, Cohen, what is there to talk about?"

There had to be a way for him to make her see reason. Women didn't just randomly pick guys up to get laid. Well, most of them didn't, he thought, remembering the barracuda who'd gone after him earlier that evening. But he wanted to believe that Dee was different. Still, hadn't she been about to hook up with Marshall? He didn't want to think about what she and the dude would be doing now if he hadn't shown up.

"It's late and you need to think about this some more. Promise me you won't do anything stupid." When she glared at him, he quickly corrected himself. "I mean irrational, not stupid. Not until we talk."

She began tapping her feet and his gaze was drawn to those killer red stilettos. When he glanced back up to her face, she was tapping a finger against those red luscious lips. Damn, red dress, red shoes, red lips. He'd bet her bra and panties were red too.

"Okay," she finally said. "I'll sleep alone tonight and we'll talk in the morning. But I can't imagine what you think you can say to make me feel better."

He didn't know either, but he intended to come up with something. "Come on, I'll walk you to your room."

She lifted her chin. "Why? So you can find out where it is and spy on me, keeping watch over who's coming and going?"

He didn't like the thought of her hotel room having a damn revolving door. "No. I want to walk you to your room because it's the gentlemanly thing to do."

"Umm, that's sounds like something Marshall would say."

He frowned, not liking the comparison. "Don't you trust me?"

"I think the question you should be asking yourself, Cohen, is…do you trust me?"

Not waiting for a response, she walked off.

**

Dee continued toward the bank of elevators. She didn't have to look behind her to know Cohen was following close behind. The heat she felt on her backside made her aware of just what part of her anatomy was holding his attention. Currently, it was a toss-up between her backside and her legs.

She intended to make his eyeballing worth his while, so she deliberately walked with a sensuous strut. Not only was Cohen noticing, but several men loitering in the halls had turned to stare as well. Let them look. The more the merrier. Hopefully Cohen would see that others desired her, even if he was fighting against it, himself.

She smiled. Things were working out rather nicely. All she had to do was continue this ruse, to see how far she could push him before he...

What?

Volunteered to take care of her needs himself? Her smile widened at the thought. When she came to the elevators, she stopped. He came to stand beside her. "Did I tell you how nice you look?" he asked.

She wished he hadn't. She glanced over at him to see him staring intently at her face, her lips. Feeling a little naughty, she deliberately licked them as if they were dry. She saw the effect of her actions when he forced air from his nostrils.

"Thanks, Cohen. You look nice yourself. But like I said, you don't have to see me up to my room."

"I know I don't have to. I want to."

"Suit yourself."

The elevator opened and they both stepped inside. A part of her was a little disappointed when a few other people got on. Instead of telling him her floor, she pushed the button on the panel wall, then moved to the other side of the elevator so it looked like she was alone.

When one of the single men in the elevator eased up beside her and asked her name, Cohen moved to stand beside her. "She's with me," he told the guy.

The stranger had the decency to apologize as he backed up. "Sorry, I didn't know."

"Now you do."

The guy quickly moved away. Dee narrowed her gaze at Cohen. She wondered if he realized he was acting more territorial than protective. When the elevator door opened on her floor, she stepped off and Cohen followed right behind her. When the door shut behind them, she frowned at him. "I am *not* with you, Cohen."

"Yes, you are."

She rolled her eyes. "Not the way you meant."

"He didn't have to know that."

"Why not let him know? I'm here and I'm available. It's not like I'm hiding anything."

"Maybe you should be," he said, deliberately looking at her cleavage.

"The girls are disappointed," she said, as she began moving toward her room.

He walked beside her. "What girls?"

"My breasts. You know, the girls."

"Oh. And why are they disappointed?"

"I had planned for a man's mouth to be doing all sorts of wicked things to them tonight."

He stopped walking and she was certain he'd nearly tripped. "Will you stop saying stuff like that?"

"Why? It's only you. I wouldn't talk like that around another guy. But with you I can be myself, you know, let my hair down, though I don't have much now," she said, shaking her short curls. "Still, you get the picture."

"Yes, I get it. But I'd rather you not talk like that around me, either."

"Why? Can't you handle a little naughty talk?"

"What you're saying is not naughty. It's provocative."

She came to a stop in front of the door to her room. "Oh, I get it. Men can talk dirty but women can't. Sounds pretty sexist to me."

He didn't say anything while she pulled the passkey out from her purse. No doubt he was still trying to figure her out. Good.

"Okay then, call me for breakfast. But not too early. Goodnight."

Then she then slid the passkey into the lock, opened the door and stepped inside…then closed it shut in his face.

10

Cohen stood rooted in place for a minute. Should he be surprised she hadn't invited him in? Had he expected her to?

She was doing the right thing. He had no business being in her room. No man did, for that matter. Why couldn't she have come here just to enjoy the beach? Read by the seashore? He would gladly take her into town to find a book store. Surely, there had to be a few books that would hold her interest.

He moved away from the door, in case she was watching him through the peephole. At least now, he knew where her room was located. Lucky for him, it wasn't too far away from his. Same side of the building, just different floors. She was on the tenth floor and he was above her on the eleventh.

Above her...

Why did just thinking that conjure up erotic images in his mind? Hell, he wasn't the horny one here. She was. And he intended to help her handle it. But how? He knew several ways of controlling male urges but had no idea about how a woman was supposed to control hers. And Dee had shared some pretty vivid needs with him over the last few days. She'd been too open, too upfront, to damn revealing. Women didn't say stuff like that to men, even those they trusted.

As Cohen went to his room, he thought about the guy on the elevator earlier, the one who'd assumed Dee was alone. He really couldn't blame the man for hitting on her. Tonight, Dee had been seduction personified. The minute she had walked into the ballroom, men had taken notice. Why did she have to look so damn seductive? Even now, he was still aroused. Then again, she'd pretty well told him that her breasts needed some attention, and that she dreamed of having his tongue on her. *Jeez.* His throat tightened and he could barely catch his breath.

Two hours later, he'd showered and was kicking back on his balcony with a beer from the bar in his room. Why was he still up at close to two in the morning? Why was he wondering what Dee was doing, wondering if she'd changed her mind and had someone with her in her room?

He shook his head. She didn't. She'd given him her word, right? In all actuality, she really hadn't, he thought before downing another mouthful of beer. She'd only agreed to talk with him in the morning.

What would he say when they met? Hell, he'd never had to deal with this kind of situation before. He needed help. Advice from someone who would know.

He then thought about Tyson. His best friend was an expert when it came to females. Luckily, Cohen knew Tyson was working the late shift at the hospital this week. He reached for his phone and hit Tyson's number.

"Hey Cohen. What are you still doing up?"

"Pondering something. I have a 'what-if' situation that I could really use your help with."

"Okay."

"Hypothetically speaking," he said.

He heard Tyson's chuckle. "Okay, hypothetically speaking."

Cohen smiled. They both knew there wasn't anything hypothetical about it. Tyson knew why he'd come here--to keep Dee out of trouble. "What if the person I'm trying to keep safe from the wolves is determined to act like Little Red Riding Hood?"

"Umm, then you need to become a more proactive wolf."

A proactive wolf? "I don't understand. What do you mean?"

"I mean that evidently, Little Red doesn't have a problem with the idea of being gobbled up. So you might as well be the wolf that enjoys the meal."

Cohen almost fell out of his chair. "Come again?"

"Think about it, Cohen. Have you considered the reason for Dee's strange behavior? You rejected her."

"I didn't reject her. I just refused to be set up for any more seductions."

"To a woman, that's basically the same thing. So now, she wants to seduce any man *but* you. She's been there, done that. Got rejected for her efforts. So now, she's looking for a guy who will appreciate her."

Hell, he'd appreciated her. He'd made love to her and would still be making love to her, if he hadn't come to his senses. "I don't want another guy to touch her, Tyson."

"Then you need to determine why. You can't give her the kind of love you think she deserves, yet you don't want another man to love her, either. That's just wrong."

"The men she's targeting are all players--carefree, love 'em and leave 'em types. Stone cold womanizers."

"Oh. The kind of men Galen, Jonas, Eli and I used to be, before finding the right girl?"

Cohen rolled his eyes and took another swallow of beer. "You know what I mean."

"Yes, I do. But have you considered that she might find a keeper in the group?"

"And she might find someone who'll break her heart."

"If you ask me, her heart is already broken," Tyson said. "Sounds like she's looking for someone to mend it."

Cohen drew in a deep breath. "Are you suggesting that I seduce Dee?"

"From the way it sounds, either you seduce her or someone else will. Which is it going to be?"

**

Dee couldn't sleep, but it was too late to call Stacey. So here she was, at two in the morning, playing a game on her smartphone. And winning. Why couldn't she win with Cohen? Why did the man have to make things so difficult?

In a way, it wasn't that she couldn't sleep. She just refused to try. Each time she closed her eyes, she would see Cohen. But not as he'd looked last night. Instead, her mind would conjure up remembered images of him naked, in her bed. She'd always thought his features were the epitome of masculine beauty. And his body was a piece of perfection, with chiseled pecs, powerfully built shoulders, and an iron tight chest, sprinkled with rough hair.

McSexy is the name she often gave him in her erotic dreams. And what she'd told him earlier was true, she often dreamed of having his mouth on her. He'd appeared scandalized by her confession, but as far as she was concerned, he had needed to hear it. In all honestly, just being around him made her ache.

She smiled, recalling their conversation tonight. She hadn't pulled any punches with him. And tomorrow, she'd do the same. He might have been shocked at her brazenness...but his body had reacted. She'd seen it, each and every time. There were some things a man just couldn't hide. Whether he knew it or not, Cohen's breathing pattern changed whenever he got turned on. And knowing she was the cause of it had just encouraged her to push him harder.

When she saw him in the morning, she intended to be even naughtier. Like she'd told Stacey, she was going to drive him crazy with lust. It was time for him to either fish or cut bait. If he didn't want her to get laid by someone else, then he needed to do the honors himself. Not that she was really looking for someone else, mind you, but she intended to make him think that she was.

So right now, her plan was to put erotic pictures in his head, images of her getting her brains screwed out while engaging in wild, hot, endless sex with a man whose face she wanted to be his. She hoped he wanted it to be his, too. If all she could get was noncommittal sex now, that would be okay. It would lead to committed sex later. She was willing to take it one step, one stroke, one hard thrust at a time.

She tightened her legs together when certain thoughts raced through her mind. She couldn't wait for the morning to come. Right now, though, she needed to make him believe she desperately wanted a man in her bed, any man.

When she'd closed the door on him last night, she had watched him through the peephole. He'd actually looked stunned. Had he thought she would open herself up to rejection a third time?

But she was holding her ground. If he wanted her, he'd have to take her. She wasn't going to offer herself up to him this time. It was his turn to be the seducer. And she intended to make him work for it.

Drawing in a deep breath, she put her phone down. She needed to be well-rested if she was going to match wits with McSexy tomorrow.

**

With very little sleep but a determination to keep Dee out of trouble spurring him on, Cohen knocked on her door at seven the next morning. He wasn't taking any chances that he'd miss her. He had no intention of letting her go downstairs without him.

He heard the security chain being moved back just seconds before the door opened. And there she stood. He was certain his jaw dropped. She'd just stepped out the shower. Sprinkles of water dotted her skin. He wondered if she was aware that a towel only covered so much, and at times, almost nothing at all. This was one of those times.

"Come back in fifteen minutes." She closed the door in his face.

He blinked, drew in a deep breath and knocked again. Moments later, she opened the door once more. "What do you want, Cohen? As you can see, I just stepped out of the shower. I need to get dressed."

"Yes, I can see that," he said, fighting to keep his gaze on her face and not shift lower. "Why can't I wait for you in there?"

She rolled her eyes. "There's not enough room."

"I can sit out on the balcony. That way, I'll be here once you're ready to go."

She gave him an impatient look before stepping aside to let him in. "Suit yourself. Just don't get in my way. I intend for today to be a good day for me."

He wondered what her definition of *good* was. "I'm looking forward to a good day, as well," he said, though he doubted she'd heard him. She'd rushed back into the bathroom and closed the door.

GUILTY PLEASURE

He inhaled deeply. The room held her gardenia scent. Glancing around, his gaze shifted to her bed. Immediately, he visualized her in it, stretched out, naked beneath the covers, trying to find a comfortable position to sleep. Then he started wondering what she slept in. A short nightgown? Long? Lacy? Sheer? Cotton? Maybe nothing at all. Did she sleep in the nude?

Knowing that following that train of thought would get him in trouble, he quickly moved toward the balcony. Since he knew Dee didn't drink coffee, he had stopped at one of the resort's cafes and bought his own. He eased into a chair and looked around. She had a beautiful view of the ocean.

This was a really nice place. He wondered how she'd found out about it. Then again, it *was* a singles' resort. How many of them could there be in Virginia Beach? Still, Cohen didn't have to think too hard to figure out why she'd selected this one...in addition to the obvious. She was surrounded by kids all year. He could certainly understand her wanting to be around adults for a change. He felt the same way. After hanging around medical professionals all day, he certainly wouldn't want to vacation with them, as well.

His ears perked up at the sound of Dee moving around. She'd come out of the bathroom. Trying to clear his mind of images of a naked Dee getting dressed, he glanced down at the view below. It was early, yet people had already begun migrating to the beach. A few were even in the water taking a morning swim, which accounted for the number of lifeguards on duty.

He shifted his thoughts to the conversation he'd had last night with Tyson. His best friend's suggestion had pretty much kept him up most of the night. Could he do it? First, though, he'd try one more time to get Dee to change her mind on her own. Then, only as a last resort, would he consider Tyson's suggestion.

"I'm ready, Cohen."

He stood and turned to look at her. Blood rushed to his face...and further south. Crossing his arms over his chest, he said in a firm voice, "No. I don't think so."

11

Dee fought hard, really hard, to keep her face from breaking into a grin. She had definitely pushed the envelope with this outfit. The look on Cohen's face was priceless. He was gawking, almost shocked out of his pants. She hadn't thought that the outfit was that bad, although she'd known once he saw it, he'd think so. In actuality, it was a two-piece sheer outfit. But to get a rise out of him, she'd put on the top without the bottoms. She would never wear something like it in public...but he didn't need to know that.

"What do you mean, you don't think so?" she asked, with staged affront, while trying not to notice how sexy he looked in a pair of shorts and a sleeveless muscle shirt.

"Just what I said. You can't wear that down to breakfast."

She crossed her arms over her chest, knowing it would cause two things to happen--make him notice her breasts, how exposed the nipples were, as well as cause the hem of the outfit to rise up even higher on her thighs. "Why not?"

He glared at her. "I can't believe you're asking me that, Dee."

"I don't understand your attitude, Cohen. I told you what I'd planned to do while I was here. So I went shopping for clothing I knew would do the job I needed them to do—draw male interest."

"You're not doing that on my watch," he all but growled.

She lifted her chin. "You don't have a watch. I'm not a child, Cohen. Take a good look."

The only bright spot in all of this was that she knew he *was* looking. His gaze raked over her from head to toe. She could tell that the man in him might like the outfit, might even find it sexy as hell. However, the Cohen in him didn't want to see it, not on her.

"I am looking Dee and this is not you."

She rolled her eyes. "Oh? How would you know? You have this image of me as a kid, Stacey's best friend, and you can't see beyond it. Well, guess what? I've matured into a woman right before your eyes. By the way, Stacey isn't a kid anymore, either. She's married and about to become a mom." She shook her head. "I really don't understand why you can't think of me as a woman."

"I do think of you that way, Dee. How could I not, after what we did together?"

Dee's chest tightened and nerves danced in her stomach. This was the first time he'd ever mentioned their nights together. Usually, she was the one who brought it up. And why did the tone of his voice hold a tenderness that nearly made her sink to her knees? More than anything, she hoped he was finally starting to see the truth—that they belonged together.

"Then what's the problem, Cohen? You awakened desires in me." *That was true.* "You've awakened a need." *That was true, too.* "So what am I to do when those desires and needs consume me? You were my first lover and so far, you've been my only one. That's turning out to be a problem for me. I see you and I want you, even knowing I can't have you. You've made that absolutely clear. So what else can I do but shift my attention elsewhere?"

He didn't say anything for a long moment. Her admission of having not been with anyone else obviously gave him pause. Hopefully, he finally got it. But if her plan was to work, hope wouldn't be enough. She needed to drive home the fact that though he'd been her first, he might not be her last...unless he did something about it. "What do you expect me to do, Cohen?"

He rubbed his hand down his face. Whether he'd done it in frustration or as a way to stop staring at her outfit, she wasn't sure. He then forced his gaze to her face, and off her chest and thighs. This particular outfit immediately drew attention to those places. She was well aware that not only were her nipples poking out from the top, but also the juncture of her thighs was shadowed, leaving it questionable as to whether or not she was wearing panties.

"Let's discuss this over breakfast, Dee. There has to be a solution and together, we'll find one."

Together they would find one... Umm, that would be interesting. "Okay, let's go downstairs, then."

"*After* you change into something more suitable."

She'd known that was coming. Still, it wasn't as if she'd actually go downstairs dressed like this. So, she capitulated. "Okay, I'll change. But only because I'm hungry and don't want to waste time fussing with you. I'll be right back."

She then turned and went back into the room. She heard him groan when he finally saw the back of her outfit. It was all lace and barely covered her butt cheeks.

She'd never had more fun in her life.

**

Cohen dropped into his chair the moment Dee left the balcony. *Holy shit!* What was he going to do? Today, he felt every bit of his thirty-seven years. How in the hell was he supposed to find a solution regarding these urges he'd awakened in her?

He couldn't just tell her to pretend they didn't exist. And he definitely couldn't let her find her own solution to her problem. God, her outfits were outrageous! The thought that she would have actually worn something like that out in public was alarming. He was used to seeing Dee in high heels with nice clothes, a typical schoolteacher. He'd never seen her in anything near as daring as what she'd been wearing lately. If she was trying to make a point, he got it. But what did he do about it?

He thought again of Tyson's suggestion. Could he become involved with Dee again, just to save her from the less desirable guys here? What would happen when they returned to their respective cities and her urges continued?

Worse, what if he started to fall for her? He wasn't sure he could sleep with her over and over again and feel nothing but sexual satisfaction. Thanks to Amanda, he'd always thought he was immune to love. She had destroyed that for him. But in this situation, he wasn't absolutely certain.

"Okay, I'm ready."

He was almost afraid to look. He let out a deep sigh of relief when he saw that Dee had put on a pretty printed sundress. It was short, but compared to what she'd had on earlier, it was decent. "Okay then, let's go."

Cohen wished he could say the trek from her room to the café on the first floor was uneventful, but it wasn't. Men still followed her with their eyes. When a woman had legs like Dee's, a guy couldn't not look. He got it, although he didn't like it.

The café was slightly crowded and it was a while before the waitress came and took their order. He just wanted another cup of coffee, but Dee ordered a full breakfast-- pancakes, sausages, eggs and hot tea.

After the waitress delivered their drinks, Dee said, "I know you said you didn't come here for yourself, but I wish you had, Cohen."

Her statement gave him pause. "Why?"

"Because you work too hard. Stacey mentioned that this was the first vacation you've had since taking that job in Florida."

He shrugged. "I flew back for both Jonas's and Tyson's weddings."

"I'm not talking about flying in one day and out the next, which is probably what you did."

Guilty as charged, he thought, taking a sip of his coffee. "I like staying busy."

"Yes, but there has to be some balance. You need to relax more."

"Possibly."

"You do."

Maybe she was right. He did need to take things easier. For years, he'd prided himself on being Stacey's older, protective brother. Now that she was married, Eli would look after her. And Cohen had to admit, the man was doing a fantastic job. Stacey had all the things he'd ever wanted for her--a good life and a man who adored her.

With Stacey no longer his worry, he should be able to chill. But he couldn't. And the main reason he couldn't was sitting directly across from him. Dee wasn't the only one with desires and needs. He had them, too. She would probably find it hard to believe, but he wanted her possibly even more than she wanted him. But she deserved more than a noncommittal sexual relationship...and that was all he could offer her.

"So let's talk about my problem, Cohen."

He drew in a deep breath, glad they were sitting at an empty table in the back. "Okay, let's start by you telling me what you want to get out all of this."

"Great sex, for starters."

He almost choked on his coffee, actually having to cough a few times to clear his throat. He picked up a glass of water and took a sip. "Great sex?"

She nodded. "Like what we had...before you got to feeling all guilty and stuff."

He cleared his throat again. "There has to be something you want, other than great sex." He had to force the last two words past his lips.

"Not really. I'm not ready for marriage or anything serious. My hopes for anything like that ended with you."

She'd said it so matter-of-factly, as if that was the way things had been, but she'd since moved on.

"You don't see marriage in your future?"

"I didn't say that. I'm just not ready for it now. I want to have fun, enjoy life. Kick up my heels."

And obviously, her legs, he thought but didn't say the words out loud. "And you don't have a problem sleeping with different men?"

"Does it ever bother you, or any man, when he sleeps with different women?"

"I'm not talking about me, Dee. I'm talking about you."

She took a sip of her tea. "I guess in my mind, I don't see them as men."

He found that odd. "How do you see them?"

"They're a means to an end. I want great sex and hopefully, they'll give it to me."

"And there's no way I can talk you out of this?"

"Not unless you know of a way to help me calm my urges."

He wasn't ready yet, to talk about the solution he'd come up with, thanks to Tyson. "Since our last encounter, have you not dated?"

"Sure. I've gone out with a lot of guys. But at the time, I wasn't ready to be touched by any of them."

Maybe he shouldn't ask, but he had to know. "Why?"

She drew in a deep breath and met his gaze. "Because their hands weren't your hands, and I knew their touch would be different. It wouldn't feel the same. You were my first and I was pretty hooked on how you'd made me feel. The sensations were all so new to me. Even my toy boyfriend, who's been with me since…"

And then, as if she'd caught herself from divulging something she shouldn't, she finished, "for a while, couldn't compare. You were simply amazing, Cohen."

He tried to keep his chest from swelling. There was no hope though, for the erection pressing against the fly of his shorts. "You just thought so because you had nothing to compare it with."

"True, but I doubt it would have mattered if I had. Still, you've made it clear we're done. So I've moved on. I guess I'll soon be able to compare now."

He didn't like the sound of that. "I recall both times, you said you loved me," he said, addressing the subject that had bothered him the most. He hadn't wanted her to waste her love on him when he'd known he could not return it. But if he decided to go with Tyson's suggestion, he needed to make sure she no longer loved him. The last thing he needed was for her to get great sex confused with love. He didn't love her and wouldn't love her, no matter how great the sex was.

She didn't say anything for the longest time. Then she met his gaze. "I did. At the time."

"But you don't anymore?"

"Honestly? Do you really expect me to still love you, after what you said to me? After all the regret, all the guilt?"

She was right. "No, I don't."

"Good, because I don't."

She'd said it as though the very thought was distasteful. That was good, wasn't it? "I hope I didn't ruin things for you, Dee."

She lifted a brow. "Ruin things, how?"

He waited until the waitress had left before answering. "First love can be a powerful thing, and if handled in a negative way, it can leave scars. Deep scars. It can affect you both mentally and physically."

"Negative, as in rejection?" she asked.

"Yes, or betrayal."

She didn't say anything for a minute, then shrugged her shoulders slightly. "I didn't feel betrayed, Cohen. I didn't have any claim on you." She chuckled. "Silly me, I actually thought I could seduce you into loving me. How crazy was that? I know better now. A person will either love you or they won't. Sex has nothing to do with it."

He didn't say anything. Instead he watched her eat, and found himself actually getting turned on by it. And as he sat there, sipping his coffee, he couldn't help noticing a few things--like the smooth way her mouth touched the rim of her tea cup whenever she took a sip. Or how every so often, she would lick her lips. Or the graceful way she held her fork.

"Sure you don't want anything? You're looking at my food as though you might take it from me any minute."

He smiled. He hadn't been checking her food out, he'd been checking her out. "I'm sure."

"You know what I regret most about making love with you, Cohen?"

Wow. Where did that come from? "No. What?"

"You never held me in your arms, afterwards. You were too busy feeling guilty about making love to take advantage of one of the best parts of it.

He felt a swift kick in the gut. He'd cheated her out of something really special, the time when he should have held her and told her how great things had been, how wonderful she was. He wished now that he'd given that to her.

"So Cohen, what do you suggest? You know why I came here. Do you intend to stand in my way?"

He knew there was only one way to stop her. Tyson was right. He would have to become proactive. At least, he knew now that she no longer loved him, which was a good thing. However, he wasn't sure how she would feel about engaging in an affair with him. Having him take care of her needs.

His suggestion might sound selfish on his part and maybe it was. But he couldn't think of any other way. In the end, he would be saving her from herself. He had to believe that. "I happen to know a guy who's staying here who might be able to help. He looks okay."

"Just okay?"

He shrugged. "I think he will do."

She took another sip of her tea. "So, what are you doing? Playing matchmaker? Pre-approving my bed partners? Don't you think I can make the decision myself?"

He could pick up on the agitation in her voice. "I'm trying to introduce you to someone who can truly help, the only person I believe who will have your best interests at heart."

She didn't say anything for a minute, then looked up at him. "Tell me more about this guy you want me to meet."

"He's not looking for any kind of serious involvement. Like you, he just wants to enjoy his time here and take the edge off."

"By taking the edge off, you mean take care of his urges, right?" she asked, as if for clarification

"Yes. The same way you want to do it."

"With great sex?"

"Yes, great sex, with no strings attached." He'd figured she would be jumping up and down at the thought about now, but she wasn't.

"Can he deliver?"

She *would* want to know that. "Yes, I think he can, but it will be up to you to find out for sure. Just so you know, he's seen you and he thinks you're hot."

"Really?" she asked dryly.

She sure didn't sound excited about it. "Yes. But he wants to make sure you understand—he doesn't intend to fall in love. It's not going happen for him, no matter how much the two of you might end up liking each other, or how great the sex is. He doesn't want to get tangled up with a woman who equates great sex with undying love."

She shook her head. "He has nothing to worry about." She took another sip of her tea. "So who is this guy? When can I meet him?"

A part of him was disappointed that she'd even consider taking him up on his offer, that she'd sleep with someone just because Cohen had vetted him. She should want more. She deserved more. But if she wasn't ready for more right now then...

He drew in a deep breath. "You can meet him now, Dee. Because you're looking at him."

12

Dee's breath caught in her throat. "You?"

"Yes. Me."

Dee was shocked. When he'd first started talking about this guy he wanted her to meet, she'd felt disheartened. He was going to hand her off to someone else. She'd had no idea he'd been talking about himself. But now that he'd told her, it made perfect sense. At least, she knew it did to him.

She had wanted to drive him so crazy, he'd seduce her. But what he was suggesting was even better. A full-fledged affair for two weeks. At the end, he intended for her to walk away, her sexual urges satisfied. And there was no doubt in her mind that they would be. But then what? Would *he* be able to walk away as easily as he expected her to do? She hoped not. In fact, she intended to do everything in her power to make sure of it.

"So Dee, how do you feel about me and you getting together?"

She was elated, but there was no way she was telling him that. Nor would she give him the idea that she'd rush into anything with him. Being too eager would throw up red flags. "Truthfully, I'd prefer a stranger, Cohen. Someone I don't know."

"Why?"

"Because there'd be less talk and more action in the bedroom. A stranger would know to do that."

"You think I wouldn't?"

"Think about it, Cohen. We have a history. We know each other too well. You would feel the need to talk, to balance things out. I don't want balance. I want great sex."

"And that's what you'll get."

She gave him a dubious look. "All the time?"

"Whenever you want."

She took another sip of her tea. "Aren't you afraid of what our families will think?"

"How will they know, unless you tell them? Stacey might suspect something, though I'm sure she already does, since Eli knows I'm here. Have you talked to her?"

"Not since I left Phoenix." And that was the truth.

"Any other concerns?" he asked her.

No concerns, but she did have questions. "I loved you, before. Aren't you worried I might fall back in love with you? That an affair with me, the kind you're describing, might get emotionally messy?"

Cohen had considered that. However, finding out she no longer loved him eased his concern. He shook his head. "Are you worried?"

"No."

"Then I'm not worried, either. You said you've moved on and I believe you. I don't think we have to worry about you falling for me again."

"Why?"

"Considering our past, I think I'd really have my work cut out getting you to forget everything I've done and fall for me again. I don't intend to do that. I'm only in it for the sex, to give you what you want and need."

"How generous of you."

Her words seemed to have a biting edge to them. "Let's not get anything twisted, Dee. I'm not doing you any favors. I have needs, myself. And unlike you, I prefer not getting it on with a stranger."

"How long will this affair last?"

"The two weeks that we're here. And it will be exclusive."

She let that sink in for a moment. "Why are you doing this, Cohen? Honestly?"

He leaned over the table, moving closer to her, desperately needing her to hear his words. "Because I don't want any other man touching you but me."

He saw the widening of her eyes and decided he needed to clarify something. "At least, not until you realize that you made a mistake in coming here. This isn't you, Dee. Once we're back home, we'll go about our lives in a more sensible way."

He eased back in his chair, satisfied that he'd expressed his feelings. "So, what do you think?"

"Your proposal sounds enticing but…"

"But what?" he asked.

"But it also sounds controlling."

He lifted a brow. "Controlling?"

"Yes. It's like, I sleep with you or no one. Like you're so sure I'd be making a mistake if I took up with anyone else."

Of course he was sure of it. "And you don't?"

"It depends."

"On what?" he asked.

"How good you are in bed."

He frowned. "You said you enjoyed making love with me," he reminded her.

"Yes, but that's when I was in love with you. It might be different now. I need to think about it."

He honestly tried to keep a straight face. Her logic showed just how inexperienced she was. Love had nothing to do with the pleasure a man and a woman could share in the bedroom. "Then think about it. I definitely don't want to rush you into doing anything. However, in the meantime, I think we need to agree on a few things."

"Like what?" she asked.

"That you don't flirt or try to catch any other man's attention."

She nodded. "That's fair."

"And that you dress decently. You don't have to attract so much attention anymore."

"That's only if I agree to your proposition. But if it makes you feel better, I will consider your suggestion. I can't make any promises, though."

He started to argue but decided to leave the situation alone for now. He would give her time to think about it, but in the end, he would win. He'd make sure he was the only man in her bed, one way or another. "So what do you have planned today?"

"I had hoped to spend my day in a stranger's bed or have him spend his day in mine."

He leaned back in his chair. "That won't happen. Unless, of course, you agree to my proposal. Then you can spend your day in mine." Why did he like the sound of that?

She placed her fork down and held his gaze. "I haven't agreed to anything yet. And until I do, I will not share my cookies."

Cohen couldn't help but smile. He liked this side of Dee. The say-whatever-I-want Dee. "Your girls, your cookies. Any other monikers I need to know about."

"None for now."

"Since sleeping together isn't an option today, is there anything else you'd like to do?"

Her eyes lit up. "Yes. I've always wanted to go parasailing."

He nodded. "Then parasailing it is."

**

It was late afternoon when Dee and Cohen returned to the resort. They'd been gone most of the day. After breakfast, they had returned to their individual rooms and changed into something more suitable for parasailing.

Today had been a lot of fun. This had been her first time trying the sport , and she'd totally fallen in love with it. Cohen had admitted that he'd tried it once before, when he'd joined the Steele brothers on one of their yearly outings. Still, she had thoroughly enjoyed herself and believed Cohen had as well. What a great day!

She checked her watch as he walked her back to her room. He hadn't mentioned anything about the proposition he'd made at breakfast, and she figured he was keeping his word about giving her time to decide.

"You want to take a nap before dinner?" he asked.

"That would be nice."

"There's a cook-out later on the beach. Do you want to go?" Cohen inquired.

"Why not? It will be fun."

He leaned against her door. "Think you'll be ready in an hour?"

She chuckled. "Let's make it two. I do need that nap."

"Okay."

McSexy was staring at her mouth. She'd noticed he'd done that a lot today. Was it the color of her lipstick or the shape of her mouth that attracted him? "I'd better go. I suggest you get some rest, as well. It was a busy day."

Dee pulled her passkey from the pocket of her shorts. "See you later." She was about to unlock her door when he reached out and touched her arm. She turned back to him. "Yes?"

That was all she could say before he lowered his mouth to hers. Dee knew her sanity was about to take a beating the moment Cohen's tongue touched hers. Then, as if taking ownership, he began sucking on hers with a hunger she felt all the way to her toes. He tasted like the strawberry candy she'd seen him pop into his mouth earlier. He wrapped his arms around her so tight, she could sense the hardness of her nipples pierce his chest. He didn't seem to mind and deepened the kiss at the same time he shifted his stance, allowing her to feel the magnitude of his engorged sex nestling between the warmth of her thighs.

Somewhere, they heard the ding of the elevator and he broke off the kiss, slowly lifting his head and holding her gaze. The intensity in his dark eyes made her heart pound in her chest. "Go on inside, now," he said in a deep throaty voice. "Enjoy your nap."

Drawing in a much-needed breath, she quickly turned to unlock her door. She glanced over her shoulder and met his gaze. "I'll see you at seven."

At his nod, she went into the room and closed the door behind her. Before she could stop herself, she took a look through the peephole. He was still standing there, staring at the peephole as if he knew she was looking. And then, he slowly licked his lips with his tongue. Heat settled in the pit of her stomach. Was he deliberately reminding her of something else he could use that tongue for? She shivered. Cohen just smiled before walking away.

Dee turned and rested her back against the door, trying to draw in a deep breath. She was supposed to be driving *him* crazy, not the other way around. Yet he'd always been able to get her worked up, with little effort on his part. Now, that he was trying...God help her.

She hadn't expected their desire for each other to still be so intense, and the realization gave her pause. When they'd made love before, it had been wild, overpowering. There was no doubt in her mind that when they made love again, it would be just as explosive.

She also realized, without a doubt, that she still loved him. Even though her plan was to play it cool, letting him believe that sex between them would mean nothing, she knew she'd be lying. Sex with him would mean everything. It always had.

Tossing her crossbody purse on a chair, she sat on the side of the bed to remove her sandals and rub the soles of her feet. They had done a lot of walking today and he'd held her hand most of the time. It was as if he'd wanted her to feel the sparks sizzling between them. And she had.

Although she'd known Cohen for years, they'd never really talked. Not like today. He'd shared information about his work, telling her about a new medical breakthrough in the field of neurosurgery that he was excited about. She knew he loved his work, but today, she could feel it.

At some point, the conversation shifted to her. She'd told him about her upcoming year as a third grade teacher, about how much she'd miss the kindergarten class she'd taught for six years. Then they'd discussed her brother Lawyer's upcoming wedding, as well as the fact that her brother Justice was still out there, sowing his wild oats.

They'd talked about everything and anything. The economy. The upcoming elections. The chances of a war breaking out. The recent increase in gas prices. And underneath it all, the sexual chemistry between them had simmered, unrelenting.

She glanced at the clock on the nightstand. She would take a nap and be ready for Cohen at seven. But she wasn't ready to give him her answer to his proposition just yet. She wanted them to spend more quality time together before that happened. Once she agreed to his proposal, she knew they'd never get out of bed. At that point, conversation would definitely take a back seat.

It was plain to see that Cohen had erected a number of walls around his heart. She intended to make sure she had what she needed to scale every one of them.

GUILTY PLEASURE

**

The moment Cohen entered his suite, he headed right for the mini-bar. Kissing Dee had shaken him to the core. Even just spending time with her had been something else, something simply fantastic. In all the years he'd known her, he doubted they'd ever shared a real conversation.

Today, he'd seen her as more than just Stacey's best friend with the gorgeous legs who looked sexy as hell in stilettos. More than the woman who, on two occasions, had seduced the hell out of him. Today, she'd simply been Dee. Someone who enjoyed having fun, and wanted him to, as well. Someone who loved her job as a teacher as much as he loved being a neurosurgeon. Someone as dedicated to her students as he was to his patients.

Tomorrow, she'd decided, they would go snorkeling. Since neither of them had ever tried it before, they'd signed up for lessons. He couldn't believe how much he was looking forward to it. It would be an adventure. He didn't want to think about what would happen once they left this place.

He'd realized one thing today, though. While they'd been out having fun, the sexual chemistry between them hadn't lessened. It was there, just waiting for them to do something about it. Now that he'd put his proposal out there, he felt as if a weight had been lifted off his shoulders. By acknowledging the desire that burned between them, he'd found some relief. She hadn't given him her answer yet, but he was hoping she would soon. In the meantime, he would continue to enjoy her company. And he did enjoy it, more than he'd ever thought he could.

Whether she knew it or not, he'd learned quite a lot about Deidre Lewis today. He'd always known of her close relationship to her family, but had never known about the other people in her life, the people she cared about. Like the kids she mentored, who were caught up in the foster-care system. Nor had he known about the time she dedicated to teaching seniors to read. He had discovered so much about her today...and he liked what he'd learned.

He still wasn't sure what had pushed him to remain standing outside her door for a minute, knowing she was probably watching him through the peephole, or why he'd sent her a message with his tongue. His only excuse was that he'd remembered what she'd said about her dreams, and his mouth's part in them. He hoped she got the message--when she was ready, he would deliver. Hopefully, that would influence her decision.

A short while later, as he sat out on his balcony drinking a scotch, he realized that he could still sense Dee's taste, even after the strong drink. It was there, on his lips, mouth and tongue. He closed his eyes for a minute and thought about how Dee had looked last night. The sexy lady in red. And then, how she'd looked today, wearing a pair of khaki shorts, a printed top and tennis shoes. Same woman. Same sex appeal. He was convinced that no matter what Dee wore, she would always grab his attention and draw him in.

And that was what worried him. He didn't want any woman to have that ability. He'd become used to protecting his heart…and his mental state. He couldn't risk falling into that black hole again.

Because the next time, he might not get out.

And that was what *really* scared him.

**

Dee looked at herself again in the full-length mirror. The outfit looked good but lacked daring. She was okay with that. The man whose attention she was trying to attract didn't need her to be daring tonight. For some reason, a part of her felt he'd want her to be just Dee.

She heard the tap on her door at exactly seven. Snapping her purse closed, she moved across the room, glanced out the peephole and then opened the door. There stood Cohen, looking sexier than any man had a right to be. He'd tilted his head just a little and was smiling at her, something she hadn't seen him do—at least, when it came to her--in a long time. He was wearing a pair of chocolate brown slacks and an off-white pullover shirt. Funny enough, she'd decided to wear a chocolate brown sundress with spaghetti straps. The border of the dress was trimmed in off-white.

"I guess you got the memo," she said, smiling brightly.

He raised a brow. "The memo?"

"Yes. The one that suggested we color-coordinate our outfits tonight."

He let his gaze roam over her, then he looked down at himself. He smiled even brighter. "Yes, I guess I did. The color looks good on us, don't you think?"

"I definitely think so." She would even go as far as to say they looked good together. She stepped out in the hall and pulled the door shut behind her. "Which restaurant are we eating at tonight?" The resort had several.

"What do you have a taste for?" he asked, as they walked toward the bank of elevators.

She was just able to resist answering "you". "It doesn't matter. I'm a big eater."

He chuckled and the rich sound flowed over her. "Yes, I found that out today. How do you eat so much and stay in shape?"

"I walk a lot and try to squeeze in aerobics whenever I can. On the days I can't make it to the gym, I work out at home with a program I found online."

"Interesting."

She glanced up and met his gaze, causing a sizzle of awareness to flow through her. At this moment, she was tempted to agree to his proposal and suggest they go back to her room and order room service. But only after they'd engaged in several rounds of mind-blowing sex.

But a part of Dee knew that there was more between them than just incredible chemistry and great sex. She knew it and more than anything, she wanted him to know it, as well. She wanted to be more than the woman he slept with, the one he thought needed him to fulfill her needs. She wanted to be the woman he trusted his heart to, the woman who would always be there for him and with him.

The sudden ding of the elevator door broke the sensuous spell. Drawing in a deep breath, she stepped inside. Somehow, she would have to find a way to control her overpowering desire for Cohen and fully concentrate on something else.

His heart.

13

Cohen thought tonight had been perfect. Dinner had been delicious. He had never had a steak he'd enjoyed more. He was a medium rare kind of guy, but without fail, his steaks were usually delivered close to being well done. But not tonight. And, he thought, glancing over at his company, he could not have asked for a more beautiful person to share the meal with. And man, did she smell good.

He watched as Dee picked up her wine glass and took a sip. His abdomen clenched and it took everything in his power to keep his breathing at a normal rate. She hadn't mentioned anything about his proposition and he wasn't sure if that was a good sign or a bad one. Even though he'd been against the idea when Tyson had suggested it, he now found himself desperately wanting her to agree to it.

He didn't miss the way men would occasionally look at her. The only good thing was that she wasn't looking back. But if she decided against his proposal, he knew she'd soon start sizing them up as possible prospects. He couldn't let that happen.

"Would you like to dance, Dee?" Even though other couples had been on the dance floor most of the evening, he had a feeling his question surprised her.

"You want to dance with me?"

He smiled. "Yes."

"But you never dance."

She was right. Normally, he didn't. But that didn't mean he didn't want to dance now. "I promise I won't step on your feet."

"No, that's not it."

"So, will you dance with me?"

It seemed that the question hung between them for the longest time. She was probably thinking the same thing he was--how it would feel to be wrapped in each other's arms, their bodies rubbing against each other?

"Yes, I'll dance with you."

He tried to keep his heart from pounding in his chest as he stood and offered her his hand. The moment they touched, a crackle of energy passed between them. He tightened his hold on her.

Then, with soulful music beating in the background, he led her to the dance floor. The overhead lights were dim, barely providing any illumination, which added to the romantic atmosphere. Cohen doubted that he needed any more stimulation. He was wired up, with hot, raw, carnal sensations filling his mid-section.

He pulled her into his arms, and immediately, desire for her had him throbbing, making him rock hard. There was no way she couldn't feel it. Feel him. And the more they swayed to the music, their bodies moving in rhythm, blood rushed through his veins and his breath caught in his throat. And if that wasn't bad enough, he'd just barely caught himself from growling in deep male appreciation at how good she felt in his arms.

Today had proven something to him, though. Even though he'd fought against it for most of his life, he had to admit--Dee was the woman he wanted. The woman he'd always wanted. He didn't have the strength or the will to turn her down again. He'd be the lover she'd always dreamed of having…if she let him.

**

Dee couldn't describe how wonderful it felt to be in Cohen's arms while they danced. Her body felt warm next to his and the scent of his masculine aftershave seemed to surround her. She couldn't help but bury her face in the hollow of his throat, drinking in more of him. This was the first time they'd ever danced together and she was amazed at how her hips and thighs flowed against his, their bodies perfectly aligned as they moved around the dance floor.

She wondered how much longer she could hold out before giving him an answer. Even now, as they danced together, they seemed to be gliding on clouds of anticipation. Ignoring the pulsating heat and carnal attraction between them was no longer an option.

But she wasn't ready to give in yet. She didn't want the decision to be hers, but his. She wanted him to take action. Although she was sorely tempted, she had to stick to her plan. She wanted him to make the first move.

Instead, he'd dropped the decision as to how things would continue between them in her lap. She wanted it in his. She had seduced him twice. Now it was his turn.

The music ended and she pulled back from the comfort she'd found in his arms. She looked up at him and the dark heat in his eyes had every hormone in her body sizzling, causing arousal to coil in her core.

"I enjoyed dancing with you," he said, taking her hand and leading her back to their table.

"And I, you." Her desire for him was at an all-time high. She feared she would give in and jump his bones if she didn't soon bring tonight to an end. She glanced at her watch. "It's getting late. We'll both need a good night's sleep if we plan to go snorkeling tomorrow."

He stared at her, as if studying her words in his mind. "All right."

He stood and offered her his hand. She took it and felt heat curl inside of her again. Her heart skipped, and then quickly began racing when he led her from the restaurant.

Dee was glad there were other people in the elevator with them as they rode it up to her room. More than once, they glanced at each other, no doubt wondering the same thing: how would tonight end? She wasn't ready to go any further than they had last night. A goodnight kiss in front of her door was all she planned on giving him. As much as she wanted to surrender to the frissons of fire and desire that were racing up her spine, at this point, it was about more than sex. It was about her love for him.

She had to admit she'd been lying--to him and to herself--yesterday when she'd told him she had fallen out of love with him. She doubted such a thing was possible. She'd loved him too much and for too long. But it was important that he believe it now. Because the last thing he'd want to do would be to hurt her in any way. And allowing her to equate good sex with love on his part would definitely hurt.

Dee had no doubt the sex between them would be good. More than good, actually. After all, it already had been. He'd made her first sexual experiences something dreams were made of. As a lover, he had catered to her every physical and emotional need, while delivering the hottest and most satisfying climaxes she'd ever imagined. Her body still simmered whenever she remembered.

After stepping out of the elevator onto her floor, he walked her to her door, holding her hand tightly in his. She wondered what he was thinking. Did he expect her to invite him in tonight? Was he wondering why she was taking so long to give him an answer?

Once in front of her door, she drew in a deep breath. "Thanks for an enjoyable evening, Cohen."

"You're welcome."

"What time do you want to meet me for our snorkeling lessons?"

"Around eight will work. That way, we can grab breakfast first."

"Okay." She reached out and cupped his cheek in her hand and on tip-toe, kissed his lips. "Goodnight."

Instead of letting her step back, he wrapped his arms around her and pulled her against his hard, solid form. She immediately felt his erection, as well as his heartbeat pounding against her chest.

He captured her mouth, devouring it in a way he'd never done before. Even the hunger she'd felt in his kiss last night didn't compare to the intensity of the one he was laying on her tonight. If he was trying to stir enough desire in her to make her change her mind and invite him in, it was working. Heaven help her, she was about to drag him into her room when the sound of the elevator door opening made her pull her mouth away.

Dee quickly regained her senses and dug her passkey from her purse. "Goodnight, Cohen."

Opening the door, she slipped inside and quickly closed it shut behind her. Then, as she'd done last night, she stared at him through the peephole. And like before, he stared back. But he wasn't frowning, as she'd expected. Instead he smiled and did the same thing he'd done last night with his tongue. Then he walked away.

She drew in a deep breath as every nerve in her body fired with potent desire. And she wondered just how long she'd be able to resist sexy Cohen Carlson.

**

Hours later, Cohen got out of bed. Slipping into the silk robe that was compliments of the resort, he decided to go sit out on the balcony. He was tired of fighting sleep. Every time he closed his eyes, he saw Dee in his bed, letting him do all the things he wanted to do to her and with her. The hottest fantasies anyone could ever imagine.

She hadn't given him her answer yet. Why? Did she not think he could give her what wanted? He knew she desired him. He saw it each and every time she looked at him, every time they touched. So, why was she hesitating? Was she unsure of herself? Of him? Did she fear a third rejection?.

Cohen rubbed a hand down his face. Maybe his proposition hadn't been a good idea, but he hadn't known what else to do. There was no way he was going to let her continue her search for a suitable sex partner, parading herself before a pack of lecherous guys who meant her no good. The thought of her sleeping with anyone else bothered him more than ever before.

He released a deep breath. Starting tomorrow, he would take matters into his own hands. Literally. It would be his hands, his mouth, his body and whatever else he needed, driving her over the edge, pushing her closer to giving him the answer he wanted.

Anticipation built in his stomach. His seduction of Dee Lewis was about to begin.

14

G ood morning, Dee."

Dee studied Cohen and wondered, not for the first time, how any man could look so delicious, so early in the morning. Today he was wearing a pair of shorts and a t-shirt. Both looked good on him. "Good morning Cohen. I'm ready," she said, stepping into the corridor and closing the door behind her. Like him, she'd decided to wear a pair of shorts. But instead of a t-shirt, she wore a printed tank top. Her bathing suit was under her outfit and she assumed his swimming trunks were under his.

"I thought we'd grab bagels and a hot drink at that small café downstairs. I don't think it would be a good idea to eat anything heavy before the lesson."

"Bagels and a cup of tea is fine with me. I'm still full from dinner last night, anyway."

"So am I. And speaking of dinner, I found a good place for us to dine tonight."

"Okay." That was one of the things she liked best about Cohen. He was a take charge kind of guy. She had no problem with him selecting a place for them to eat. So far, all the places he'd chosen--whether it had been for breakfast, lunch or dinner--had been wonderful, and the food, outstanding.

As if it was the most natural thing in the world to do, he took her hand and headed for the elevator. "Did you rest well last night?" he asked, as he pressed the button for the elevator to come up to their floor.

McSexy would have to ask. Yes, she'd rested well enough, if you wanted to count the number of erotic dreams she'd had of them together. More than once during the night, she'd awakened on the verge of an orgasm. "I did, thanks. Are you feeling relaxed, Cohen?"

He glanced down at her, his eyes, dark and penetrating. "Relaxed?"

"Yes. From taking some time off work. Do you think you'll be well rested when you return to the hospital?"

He smiled at her. "That's my plan."

She doubted Cohen knew the meaning of relaxing, so she intended to help him. She'd suggested parasailing and snorkeling. Now it was his turn to come up with ways to spend their time. "So, what do you want to do tomorrow?"

He leaned close and whispered hotly near her ear, "Umm, I'll let you figure that one out, Dee."

Before she could respond, the elevator opened. They stepped inside, joining other singles anxious to experience everything the resort had to offer.

**

"We're having dinner in your room?"

Cohen's smile slipped into a grin. He'd just arrived to escort Dee down to dinner...or so she'd thought. "Yes, my room."

"Why?"

Was that nervousness he detected in her voice? "I thought it would be a little more intimate," he said, as they walked down the corridor toward the elevators.

"Intimate?"

Yes, that *was* nervousness in her voice. "Do you have a problem with it?"

She glanced up at him. "No, I guess not."

He found it quite telling that a woman who'd snuck into his bed a few years ago would be so reluctant to be in his room. "We can always go to a restaurant if you're uncomfortable." There was no need to tell her about everything he'd done to make ensure the evening would be incredible for both of them.

She shrugged delicate shoulders. "Why would I be uncomfortable?"

Good question. "You seem nervous."

"You're imagining things."

"Okay." He paused a minute, then attempted to lighten the mood. "Did you enjoy snorkeling this morning?"

"Oh, yes. I definitely want to do it again, sometime. What about you?"

"I really liked it," he replied honestly. First off, he'd seen her in that two-piece swimsuit. All those luscious curves contained in a bikini so skimpy, he thought it unsuitable for public display. Luckily, he'd signed them up for private lessons. He wasn't sure he could have handled watching her be ogled by a whole bunch of men. She was his to admire. Still, he was grateful she'd put her shorts and top back on before leaving the area where the lessons had been held. It had been hard enough for him to concentrate on what the snorkeling instructor was saying. He couldn't take his eyes off Dee.

Then there was her company. It was nice spending time with someone he knew so well already. He liked that she was independent in every way, even though she was raised with two older brothers. Over the years, he'd gotten used to being protective where Dee and Stacey were concerned, but in retrospect, he had to admit that they usually made sound decisions. The only time he'd worried about Stacey was when she'd become involved with Wallace Flowers. But then, as Stacey said, maybe some things were meant to be. Should he feel that way about his encounter with Amanda? Somehow, he just couldn't justify going through that period in his life without feeling it had been a lesson for him never to make the same mistake again, to never be so careless with his heart again.

He looked at Dee. Her decisions were usually pretty good, too. And that was why this whole singles' vacation idea of hers had thrown him so badly.

The elevator came to a stop on his floor and they stepped off. He took her hand in his again and he could feel the tension running through her. She'd said she wasn't nervous about being alone with him in his room, but her body language said otherwise.

When they reached his door, he opened it and ushered her inside. "Welcome to my room, Dee."

**

Dee noticed the table set for two the minute she crossed the threshold. The second thing she noticed was just how much larger his room was than hers. He had a spacious three room suite that included a bedroom, a living room and an eat-in kitchen combination. And his view of the ocean put hers to shame.

"Nice," she said, glancing around.

"Thanks. And nice outfit."

She glanced down at herself. She knew very well what she was wearing, but at that moment, she needed to break eye contact with him. "I bought this a few years ago. Stacey and I were on one of our shopping sprees." She had liked the flowing floral-print skirt with matching tunic the moment she'd seen it on the mannequin.

"It looks good on you." He checked his watch. "I gave room service an estimated time of delivery. Dinner should be here any minute."

"What are we having?"

"It's a surprise."

Dee wondered if their meal would be the only surprise. Although his suite was a lot larger than hers, the atmosphere was still very close. And charged.

"Would you like to check out the view from the balcony?"

"Yes, please. I noticed there is a lot more ocean to see from here."

"That's one of the reasons I selected this room," Cohen said, leading her over to the sliding glass door.

Again, his scent overwhelmed her senses. He smelled so darn good. She stepped out on his balcony and smiled. There was definitely more ocean to see from here. He'd come to stand directly behind her and placed his hands on her shoulders. His body was pressed to hers and she could feel his erection against her backside. She fought back a moan.

"So, what do you think?" he asked her.

About what? The size of the ocean or your erection? She shivered.

"Cold?"

"No, I'm fine. The view is beautiful."

"I think so, too," he said, slowly turning her around to face him. "You are definitely beautiful."

Now his erection was poking her in the stomach. She swallowed as she gazed up at his face. A mischievous grin glittered in his eyes. "I thought we were taking about the ocean," she said, feeling the sexual chemistry sizzling between them.

"Baby, we can talk about whatever you like."

Baby? Why did his use of that term of endearment have her hormones doing a happy dance? She parted her lips to ask him for the real reason they were dining in his room, but at that moment, there was a knock on their door.

He smiled and took a step back. "Dinner has arrived."

**

Cohen wiped his mouth with a napkin. The meal had been superb and he hoped Dee had enjoyed it as much as he had. He watched as she placed her fork beside her plate. He realized he'd watched her a lot during the course of the evening, but he didn't regret it. "I hope dinner pleased you."

She glanced up at him and smiled. "Everything about tonight pleased me. The salmon was prepared just the way I liked it."

He nodded as he took another sip of his wine. "So, what are you going to do for the rest of the summer, once you get back to Memphis?"

"Assist Beth anyway I can with the wedding. She doesn't have any family so Mom and I are helping out. I understand you're going to be there."

"I will. I can't believe Lawyer is finally tying the knot. Maybe Justice won't be too far behind."

Dee chuckled. "Don't hold your breath. Justice is having too much fun running around. He's a player."

He remembered what Tyson had said a few nights ago. "Even players settle down when they find a good woman."

"Does that mean you'll settle down someday?"

He was surprised by her question. "I don't consider myself a player." That much was true. He could go months without dating and it wouldn't bother him in the least. "And as for settling down, I don't see marriage in my future. Ever."

"Why?"

He looked into his wine glass, then glanced back at her. "Let's just say, I have my reasons." Wanting to change the subject, he said, "Ready for dessert?" He'd ordered key lime pie, which he knew to be her favorite.

"Yes."

"Come on. It's a nice night to sit on the balcony. We can eat out there."

"Sounds like a wonderful idea."

Cool air from the ocean drifted over him when he slid open the glass doors. She took one chair and he took the other as he placed their desserts on the table between them, along with their glasses and a bottle of wine.

"I hope you don't think I need a refill," she said, glancing at the wine bottle. "Any more and you will have to carry me to my room."

Or I can carry you to my bed, he thought, though he kept that thought to himself. "I wouldn't have any trouble taking you back to your room."

He watched as she sliced into the pie with her fork and then lifted a mouthful to her lips.

"This is really good," she said, using her fork to take another bite.

He watched her, getting turned on by her obvious enjoyment. She had such a pretty mouth. He'd thoroughly enjoyed kissed it, using his tongue to explore inside, going deep. Memories of their last kiss still made his head reel. He recalled how he'd sucked on her lower lip before greedily mating her mouth with his.

"You're not going to eat any of your pie?" she asked him.

"Why? You want some of mine?"

She chuckled. "Don't tempt me to say yes."

He met her gaze. "Can you be tempted, Dee?"

"I don't know any woman who can't be tempted. Or any man, for that matter."

He didn't say anything. For years, after that disastrous affair with Amanda, he'd thought he was above temptation. But Dee had proven him wrong. Twice, her passion and desire had overridden his caution.

"I absolutely love it here," he heard her say. "I understand Jacksonville has nice beaches, as well."

He leaned back in his chair. "I've heard that, too."

She looked at him in surprise. "You've lived there for over two years and you haven't visited the beach?"

"No. I've been busy." This conversation was making him realize just how much of a life he didn't have. He was starting to regret spending so much time at the hospital when there were places close by for him to enjoy.

"I'll take our empty plates inside," she said, standing.

"And I'll grab the wine bottle and glasses," he said, getting up at the same time.

She reached for the plates just as he reached for the glasses. Their hands touched and a jolt of pure sexual energy rocked him to the core.

She snatched her hand away. "Sorry," she said, in quavering voice.

Placing the glasses back down on the table, he reached out and took the plates from her hands, setting them down as well. "No need to apologize, Dee." He took her hand.

Tightening his fingers around hers, he eased her around the table and drew her to him. When she didn't pull away, he asked, "You know what I think?"

She shook her head and looked up at him. "No, what do you think?"

"I think it's time we both got laid."

15

Dee's heart began fluttering in unadulterated anticipation. His words weren't as romantic as she'd hoped for, but the meaning was the same. Still, she refused to think of it as anything less than making love.

She knew the score with Cohen. He'd made up his mind about falling in love. But by the time their two weeks were over, she hoped she'd have managed to tear down a piece of that wall surrounding his heart, even if she had to remove one brick at a time.

"Is that your take on things?" she asked. "That we both need sex?"

"Yes. By your own admission, you need it. And I definitely do. You have the ability to drive a man crazy with desire."

"I don't know about that, Cohen. You look pretty sane to me."

"Allow me to prove otherwise." And then he captured her mouth in a devouring kiss.

Powerful shivers of awareness surged through her while their tongues mated with an intensity that had her moaning deep in her throat. She was convinced every nerve in her body shook while a rush of sensations stroked her from the inside out. She inched closer, circling her arms around his neck while his tongue robbed her of her senses.

He slowly broke off the kiss, then used his tongue to lick one corner of her mouth. "So what do you think now?" he whispered against her lips.

"I think you're a great kisser, Cohen Carlson."

"Are you ready for me to show you that love has nothing to do with how great it can be in the bedroom?"

He was wrong. Love had everything to do with it. And by the end of these two weeks, she intended to make sure he understood that lesson. "If that's what you think."

"That's what I know."

She leaned in close, aware of him in every single pore of her body. "Then show me," she whispered.

No sooner had the words left her mouth than she was swept into his arms and carried inside his suite. "This time, I want to undress you the right way," he said, taking a step back after placing her on the bed.

It was on the tip of her tongue to tell him she didn't have a problem with the way he'd done it that last time, when he'd practically ripped off her clothes. There was a lot to be said about spontaneous sex. Maybe she could tempt him into doing it again before they left here.

She looked back at Cohen. He had removed her sandals and was gently caressing her feet as if he'd never seen them before. "Is anything wrong?"

He glanced up at her and a smile touched the corners of his lips. "No. I was just wondering how such dainty feet can look so sexy in a pair of stilettos."

His compliment warmed her inside. "Do they?"

"Yes. I remember the first time I saw you in them. My eyes never left your legs the entire time. Even when they should have."

The feel of his fingers rubbing her feet felt wonderfully sensuous. "When was that?"

"That time when you and Stacey were attending college in Ohio. I was passing through Columbus and stopped by your apartment. Stacey wasn't home and you were getting ready to go out for the evening. I had to recover from seeing you in a blue dress that I thought was way too short. But what caught my attention were the legs under that dress. It was the first time I'd ever seen you wear stilettos."

She was amazed that could remember so many details after all this time, even recalling the color of the dress…and the fact that it was too short.

"I remember that night. You surprised Stacey with your visit. And yes, I was on my way out to meet friends at a nightclub. I'm surprised you can recall so much about it."

Cohen shrugged. "I have a good memory. Now for this skirt."

He reached out and slid her skirt down her legs, tossing it in a chair across the room. That left her wearing only a pair of skimpy panties.

He chuckled. "I wondered if you were wearing any," he said, running his fingers along the waistband of her underwear.

"I always wear panties."

At his arched brow, she added, "Well usually. I admit, a few of the outfits I've worn lately don't require them."

"So I noticed."

Had he? She was beginning to realize that Cohen noticed a lot. Even when she thought he wasn't looking. Her attention was drawn back to his hands, which were now unbuttoning her tunic blouse.

"So many buttons," he muttered.

Although she really liked this outfit, it wouldn't have bothered her in the least if he'd ripped it off. But she didn't say anything. He was taking his time, and she was enjoying it. She was amazed at how composed he was. Then suddenly, she heard his sharp intake of breath, and she knew why.

"You're not wearing a bra." He sounded shocked.

"Nope." But she doubted he heard her answer. His gaze was fixated on her breasts. "You want to meet my girls, Cohen?"

He shifted his gaze to her face, and smiled. "Most definitely."

**

Cohen wanted to do more than meet them. He intended to devour them. Never had he seen a more perfect pair. Even though this wasn't the first time he'd seen Dee's breasts, it was the first time he'd allowed himself time to study them to this degree.

They were definitely the real thing, no enhancements needed. They were full, firm and the perfect size for her body. He could see why she could go without wearing a bra with some of her outfits. Her breasts were gorgeous. Even the nipples looked luscious.

He reached out and cupped them in his hands. For the moment, he just wanted to stare at them. Touch them. Study their tight fullness, their creamy brown coloring and their sexy curves. She was so well endowed. And responsive--her nipples seemed to swell before his eyes. He could imagine rubbing them against his chest, licking them all over and sucking them into his mouth.

"Cohen?"

Did he hear a quiver in her voice?" "Umm?"

"Are we going to get things started here?"

He nuzzled her breasts. "You in a rush?"

"Sort of. Why are you torturing me?

He flicked his tongue across a nipple and was pleased to hear her moan. "I just don't want to miss anything. I hope that's not a problem."

"Um, no problem."

Her breathing changed and she let out another sexy little moan. Funny, at that moment, he hadn't really given her anything to moan about. At least not yet.

**

Dee was convinced Cohen was intentionally driving her mad. No fair. That's what she was supposed to do to him. What she *had* done to him before. She knew it, even though he'd denied it. Now she was getting paid back in the most exquisite way possible. Using his tongue, he flicked her nipples, then circled them...then repeated the process, over and over. He was creating a delirious pattern that left her groaning in need.

Just when she thought she could handle the torment, he eased a nipple between his lips and began sucking on it, making her sex throb. She whispered his name. There was no way she could hold it back and she didn't try. Cohen was stirring sensations within her that she couldn't fight. Sensations she needed to feel. And Lordy, all he'd done so far was ravage her breasts. Branding them.

On instinct, she reached out and held his head to her chest when he increased the pressure of his mouth on her nipples. He was driving her to the brink of insanity, beyond the realms of reality.

Sexual excitement curled in her stomach. She felt her pulse thicken as her body began to shiver. This was slow, unadulterated agony. But she didn't want him to stop. Each stroke stimulated a deep tug in the juncture of her thighs.

Suddenly, her body exploded in an orgasm. She closed her eyes as the vibrations pushed her over the edge, her body hammered with pleasure.

"Open your eyes, Dee."

She did and he was there, just inches from her mouth. He kissed her deeply, thoroughly, making her toes curl. Then his tongue was at it again, dominating her senses. This kiss had the ability to ignite explosives in her gut.

She began trembling again and immediately felt another climax build. There was no way it could happen again, not this soon. But it was. His mouth was driving her crazy with desire. She was drowning in the taste of him.

Then it happened again, just from his kiss. The intensity of his hunger for her swept over her like a tidal wave. And she was blasted into yet another climax.

It seemed he deliberately drew out the kiss, eliciting purrs from deep within her throat. Finally, he stepped back and pulled his shirt over his head. "That's two down. Plenty more to go."

**

The look on Dee's face was priceless. She was about to find out there were many ways and degrees of making love. And that orgasms could be different, depending on the source. Some were more compelling than others, though they were all mind-blowing. She'd been a virgin their first time. Once he'd discovered that, he had been gentle and the next morning, regretful. This time around, he didn't want to be any of those things. He wanted to take her hard. And often. There would be no regrets.

He slid his slacks down his legs. Before tossing them aside, he reached into the pocket for a condom. Thinking of how good it would feel to be skin-to-skin with her, he asked, "Are you still on the pill?"

He could tell she was surprised he'd remembered. "Yes."

"I'm healthy. Mind if I don't use the condom."

A sensuous smile touched her lips and he felt his erection harden even more. "I was just about to suggest that. I'm healthy, too."

"Good. I want you to feel me coming inside of you."

Her eyes darkened. "I want that too."

But before that happened, he wanted her to feel something else--his tongue inside her, tasting her, lapping up her juices. She was looking at him, watching him strip, reacquainting herself with his body, just as he was doing with hers. His erection preened under her attention.

"So, are you ready to work some muscles?" he asked, moving back toward the bed.

"Yes."

"Good. Then open your legs."

Unashamedly, he watched as she spread them. Then, instead of mounting her as she probably thought he would, he placed both hands on her thighs and lowered his head between them.

**

At the first touch of Cohen's tongue inside her, Dee wanted to scream. This is what she needed. She had lain in bed plenty of nights reliving this. The way he'd used his tongue inside of her, as if she was the best thing he'd ever tasted.

Reaching down, she grabbed hold of his shoulders, digging her fingernails into his skin as he locked his mouth down on her, giving her one hell of an intimate kiss.

She closed her eyes and moaned. Her brain cells were scrambled and she was convinced every part of her body was about to explode. Her nipples were still hard from his attention earlier, and his mouth was causing a slow and penetrating throb to spread through her entire body.

Then it happened again…a third time in less than an hour. Waves and waves of ecstasy washed over her, through her and around her. She gasped when instead of releasing her, he locked his mouth tighter on her sex and began thrusting his tongue deeper inside her.

"Cohen!"

She was convinced her throat would eventually become raw from calling out his name. But at the moment, she didn't care. The only thing she cared about was how he was making her feel.

A short while later, still reeling from the pleasure he'd given her, she opened her eyes and saw him positioned above her. He licked his lips. "You said you often dream of me going down on you. I hope the real thing was better than any dream," he said in a husky tone.

"It was," she said, barely able to get the words out.

"Now, for the main event," he said, then captured her mouth with his. She doubted she would ever tire of being kissed by him. He made each kiss a work of unexplainable art. Each one was better than the last, and made her greedy for another. This kiss was longer, hotter, and filled with expectation.

She was so caught up that she hadn't realized he was entering her body until he was there, in one hard thrust. Pressing deeper, and then retreating, repeating the process over and over again. Stroking her in the same way he'd done with his tongue, but this time, doing it with more intensity and girth. And he went so deep...

The feel of his muscled body between her legs was tripping her pulse, making hot sparks rush through her. His male scent surrounded her. She was drowning in the essence of him, the feel of him, and she willingly gave herself up to the pleasure.

And then he suddenly released her mouth and threw his head back. She felt the fullness of his erection expand even more inside of her. She was being consumed, inch by masculine inch. His hands gripped her thighs, as if to keep her from going anywhere. Heavy-lidded eyes stared down at her as his body thrust inside of her like a jackhammer out of control.

And then it happened. To both of them at the same time.

"Cohen!"

"Dee!"

She felt him blast off inside of her. Felt his hot semen coat her insides while every bone in her body sizzled. She reached out and her hands skimmed his body. He felt hot. And that same heat was curling inside of her, all the way to her womb. She'd known in her heart that when they made love again, it would be spectacular. But this was beyond anything she'd ever dreamed of. He kept going, thrusting inside of her until she had drained everything out of him. It was only then that he slowed his body, shifting his weight off her, and pulled her into his arms.

**

Cohen wasn't sure how long he'd slept but when he woke up, he found Dee awake and staring at him. She wore an expectant look. He rubbed his hands down his face as if to wipe away the drowsiness. "What's wrong?"

"Nothing."

He knew there was. Had he hurt her? Had he been too demanding? He shifted his leg and discovered he was still inside of her. Soft, but inside of her nonetheless. At least, he *had* been soft. Now he was expanding. Getting hard. Still, he tried to focus on what was bothering her, instead of how good it felt to be inside of her.

He tightened his arms around her, tilting his body to push deeper. "Tell me, Dee. What's the matter?"

She nervously licked her bottom lip with her tongue and his stomach clenched. "I wanted to see if you would…"

When she didn't finish, he prompted. "I would what?"

"Do what you've done before. Tell me how much you regret making love to me, how guilty you feel. Then let me know that we should never do this again."

Her description of how things had gone down before made him sound like a heartless bastard. No wonder she didn't love him anymore. "No, I won't do that." He wriggled his hips, pushing deeper inside her. "Do I feel like I plan to leave you anytime soon? I happen to like where I am. In fact, I'm ready to make you come again."

He rolled on top of her, determined to show her there was no other place he rather be. Whatever guilty pleasure he'd felt before had been replaced with unabashed, shameless satisfaction. And while they were in Virginia Beach, that was just how things would be between them.

16

Over the course of the next ten days, Cohen and Dee spent the majority of their days and nights together. Waking up in each other's arms had become the norm and their walks on the beach were something they looked forward to doing every morning and afternoon. Although they spent a lot of time in bed, they spent just as much time out of it. They had perfected their snorkeling skills, had gone parasailing a few more times, had hiked in a nearby forest and had even signed up for cooking classes.

Dee loved this place and was glad she'd decided to come to Virginia Beach. She was even happier that Cohen had decided to follow her here. He was fulfilling all her needs, and then some. Still, he had yet to talk about what would happen when they left, going their separate ways. More than once, she'd been tempted to broach the subject of her visiting him in Florida, but she'd always thought better of it. She didn't want to risk losing what she had right now.

GUILTY PLEASURE

With only a few more of days left before their vacation ended, she had hoped to see more progress by now. Sure, they enjoyed each other's company, and had gotten to know more about each other lives and careers. But still, the main thing holding them together was sex. Great sex, but still... Cohen was truly a spectacular lover, unselfish, innovative and thoughtful when it came to pleasing her. She was falling deeper and deeper in love with him each day.

She had wanted to believe that she could get through to him, to show him that not all women were the same. That he could trust her with his heart. But she could tell that there was still a part of him locked away, a part he refused to open up to anyone, even her.

But she refused to give up on him. Refused to believe he didn't care more for her now than he had before. How could he not see how in tune they were with each other, how totally in sync they were, both in and out of bed.

The thought that she might have overplayed her hand bothered her. What if Cohen could never love her? What if he'd just been acting like a typical guy these past two weeks, taking what she'd so freely and unconditionally given, with no other intention than to enjoy it while it lasted?

She pushed back those thoughts. She intended to use these last three days to her advantage. One way or the other, she'd make sure that when he left here, he would know he was deeply loved, whether he wanted to be or not.

She pulled herself up in bed and looked at the clock sitting on the night stand. She figured Cohen had gone downstairs to grab breakfast. They would eat out on his balcony before starting their day with a walk on the beach.

Although they spent most of their time in his suite, he hadn't asked her to move in, so she'd kept her room. She had, however, managed to hide a few items of clothing in his closet.

It had felt so right to see her things hanging next to his. He hadn't said anything about it and neither had she. Easing out of bed, she decided to shower and get dressed. She only had a few more days with Cohen. And she needed to make them count.

**

Cohen stepped off the elevator and smiled. He'd left Dee upstairs sleeping soundly in his bed after a night of continuous lovemaking. He doubted she was aware he'd left her side to come downstairs and he couldn't wait to get back to her. He liked having her in his bed, maybe too much. But then, he liked having her out of his bed as well.

It was hard to believe they only had three days left to enjoy the beach. She'd been right. He'd needed this. He hadn't realized just how hard he'd worked over the past two years, somedays non-stop. He'd almost forgotten how it felt to relax. But Dee had helped him to unwind and had introduced him to new adventures.

She was good for him. More than once, he'd wondered if he was becoming a little obsessed with her. The only thing that helped was knowing they were in an agreed upon, uncommitted, uncomplicated arrangement.

Or did it?

He paused a moment and drew in a deep breath. No, it really didn't. Even now, he was sorting through feelings he'd rather not deal with. More than anything, he wished he could just concentrate on the here and now. But this would end in three days. Then what?

The thought of her returning to Memphis and her life there pushed him to do a reality check. Over the past two weeks, he'd discovered Dee was a very passionate woman. Sexual in every sense of the word. And she made him feel as if he was the only man she'd ever wanted. The only one she needed and desired. But what would happen when they parted ways? Would it be a case of out of sight, out of mind?

He couldn't forget the reasons he'd followed her here. She'd been reckless, driven by the need to get buck wild with any man willing to accommodate her. Would she return to that mindset once she got home, seeking out other men for satisfaction and fulfillment?

He pushed those dark thoughts to the back of his mind as he placed his order. He was antsy and couldn't wait to get back to her. When had any woman made him this anxious? A part of him worried that he'd allowed her to become so important to him. He only had eyes for her. It was as if no other woman existed.

A short while later, he opened the door to his suite and his nostrils were assailed by her luscious scent. Placing the bags on the table, he strolled to the bedroom and there she was, tidying up the bed.

She wore some of the cutest outfits and today's short set was no exception. Then again, whatever she put on her body drew attention. She just looked so damn good in her clothes. The woman was gorgeous personified.

Her back was to him. Obviously, she hadn't heard him enter. He stood there, leaning in the doorway, watching her. His heartbeats were like a steady punch in his chest. His reaction to her took him by surprise. He wasn't happy with the fact that he was allowing her to get under his skin. If he wasn't careful, she would be trampling that wall he'd erected around his heart. And though he felt something for Dee, he couldn't allow any woman to have that much power over him again. The embarrassment he'd felt at being so vulnerable was something he doubted he would ever get over.

Convinced he had regained control of his senses where Dee was concerned, he straightened and ever so slowly moved toward her. She didn't detect his presence until he was just inches away from her. She jerked around and must have seen the look of heated desire in his eyes. "I've just made the bed, Cohen."

He reached out and caressed her cheek. "I'll help you make it back up again." And then he leaned toward her and captured her mouth with his.

**

Cohen came wide awake when his cell phone rang. He knew this particular ringtone. It was from the hospital and always meant there was a medical emergency. He glanced at the clock as he quickly pulled himself out of bed. It was close to three in the morning. He reached for his phone on the nightstand. "Dr. Carlson."

"Dr. Carlson, this is Rebecca Cane from Jacksonville Memorial. I wanted to let you know that Dr. Frazier had to take an immediate leave of absence, due to a family emergency. His wife and son were involved in a car accident while visiting her parents in Arkansas. A head-on collision. There were no survivors."

"Oh no." Cohen rubbed his hands down his face. His heart immediately went out to his colleague. What a tragic loss. Bob Frazier had been one of the first people to reach out to him when he moved to Jacksonville. He and his wife Kathi had invited him to their home for dinner then, and he'd visited them often since. Five-year old Kenneth had been their only child. "I am so very sorry to hear that."

"Yes, we all are. It was such a tragedy. I know you're on vacation, but Dr. Frazier had surgeries lined up for the rest of the week. Some we can reschedule, but others are critical. We were hoping that you would consider--"

"I'll be on the next flight out," he said, knowing what she was about to ask him.

"Thank you, Dr. Carlson."

He clicked off the phone and looked over at Dee, who was awake and watching him. "I have to head back to Jacksonville immediately," he said, then filled Dee in on the situation.

"How absolutely horrible! The poor man," Dee said, getting out of bed as well.

Cohen glanced around for his clothes. Then he remembered that he'd taken his time undressing Dee in the sitting area last night. He'd left his clothes there too, right beside hers. He swiftly walked out of the bedroom and picked his clothes up off the floor. Then he grabbed his phone. "I need to find a flight out. Once I'm booked, I'll shower and pack."

"I'll go to my room and start packing as well."

Dee was sliding into the dress he'd so enjoyed taking off her last night. "No need for you to leave, too. You still have a couple of days left here before you have to return to Memphis."

She stopped. "I hadn't planned to go back to Memphis yet."

He lifted a brow as he slid into his jeans. "You going to Phoenix?"

"No. I assumed I'd be heading out to Jacksonville with you."

His hands went still on the belt he'd pulled through the hoops on his jeans. Warning bells were going off in his mind. "Going to Jacksonville with me? Why?"

She dropped down on the sofa. "If you have to ask, Cohen, then there's no reason why. Sorry, I misunderstood."

"And what did you misunderstand?"

She shrugged. "I thought we were having a good time together here."

"We were. But you do understand why I have to leave, right?"

"Yes, of course. But I was hoping things wouldn't have to end here, that maybe, they could continue in Jacksonville."

He shook his head. "I'll be too busy. Not only will I be taking over Dr. Frazier's workload for a while, but I've got my own to get back to. And right now, I don't know what his workload actually is, how many surgeries he has scheduled or his patients' conditions. I won't have time for--"

"Me. I knew that and hadn't planned to get in the way. I just thought you'd like having me there when you got off work…"

"I'm used to coming home to an empty house, Dee," he said as he finished dressing.

"I see."

He hoped she did. He didn't want to hurt her, but she needed to understand that he didn't want a woman in his life. Maybe, though things were horrible for Dr. Frazier, the call from the hospital had been a good thing for him. Because as much as he hadn't wanted it to happen, Dee had gotten under his skin. He woke up every morning anxious to see her, be with her, have her in his arms. He realized that not only did they match up perfectly in bed, but they matched up perfectly everywhere else, as well. His time with her had made him question his decision to avoid emotional ties. But he couldn't—*wouldn't*--let that happen. "We had a good time, Dee. But we both knew there was a time limit. I only agreed to help you take care of your needs for two weeks."

She lifted her chin. "I know that. But I was hoping that…"

"What? That I'd change my mind about relationships because things have been so good between us?"

"Yes. And because I gave you the chance to see that I'm nothing like Amanda."

Hearing that name was like a hard kick in his gut. He threw down the shoes he was about to put on his feet and walked across the room to Dee. "What do you know about Amanda?" he asked in a harsh tone.

"Only what I heard."

He frowned. Stacey knew nothing about his first love. He was sure of it. And he'd never mentioned her to anyone else but Tyson, whom he trusted absolutely. "Heard from whom?"

"You."

His frown deepened. There was no way that was possible, unless he talked in his sleep, which he was pretty sure he didn't do. "I would not have said anything about her to you, Dee."

"No, you would not have. You would have continued on your current path, comparing me and every other woman to her, making us pay for what she did to you."

He reached out and grabbed Dee's arm. "What the hell are you talking about?"

"I know about all about Amanda, Cohen. I was there, in the basement, when you told Tyson the whole story. I heard you."

"You eavesdropped on our conversation?" he accused furiously.

"I was there first. I'd gone down there to use the bathroom. You guys came down after I did."

"You could have let us know you were there."

"Yes," she said. "I could have. But by the time I realized what you were saying, I couldn't. Besides, it was obvious you needed to get it off your chest."

He released her arm and stepped back. "You had no right to listen in, Dee."

"Well, I did. What Amanda did was wrong. But it's also wrong for you to deny us the chance to--"

"Us? What us?" He rubbed his hand down his face. "I thought we agreed these two weeks would be purely physical, with no emotional fallout."

"You might be able to do that, but I can't. I love you."

"Love me? You don't love me. You said so."

She crossed her arms over her chest. "I lied. I've always loved you."

"I took you at your word. I would never have gotten involved with you if I'd known otherwise. I don't want your love, or anybody else's."

She dropped her arms to her side and took a step forward. "That's another mistake you've made, thanks to Amanda. You think love can be turned off and on, whenever a person pleases. That's not the way love works."

"I don't care how it works. It's not for me and I don't want any part of it."

"Too bad. You can't control my feelings. And another thing--" she said, leaning against a table. "Depression is nothing to be ashamed of."

"I don't want to discuss it."

"But I do. When I think of everything you went through, losing your father and then the woman you loved, an emotional meltdown is understandable."

"It's none of your business, Dee," he said in a voice filled with rage.

She just looked at him for a minute. Then in a calm voice, she said, "I've given you three chances to accept my love, Cohen. You've just used up the last one. I've said this before--though I really didn't mean it at the time, but I do now. I truly do... I hope you have a miserable life."

She then quickly walked out the suite and slammed the door behind her.

**

Dee entered her room, refusing to give in to tears. Damn his inability to let go and move on. She had given Cohen her love and he still refused to accept it. Instead he chose to wallow in self-pity, drowning in the pain of his past. It wasn't that she didn't have any sympathy about what he'd gone through, but she felt it was time for him to start over, to see what a great life they could share together and not hold Amanda's transgressions against her.

She had given him his last chance. She'd believed that finally, this time she'd be able to at least put a crack or two in the wall around his heart. But she'd failed...miserably.

Cohen might have a problem moving on, but Dee didn't. She knew when to throw in the towel. She loved him but was determined to find a way to eradicate him from her heart. She couldn't take the pain any longer.

The past two weeks had changed her. For the first time in years, she'd been happy and she'd thought he'd been happy, too. Not happy enough, she guessed.

Tossing her purse on the table, she walked straight to her bed and dropped down on it. Then, finally, she let go and gave in to her tears.

17

Cohen stepped off the hospital elevator. It was hard to believe that three weeks has passed since he'd left Virginia Beach. He'd been extremely busy taking on Bob's patients, as well as his own. Understandably, Bob had taken a leave of absence to deal with his grief. To ease the workload, the hospital had hired another neurosurgeon from Tampa and the doctor was working out great.

This would be the first day Cohen had left work at a reasonable hour since returning from Virginia Beach. He even had a full week off, now that things at the hospital had finally stabilized. But no matter how many hours he worked or how tired he was, he couldn't stop thinking about one particular woman.

Dee.

Even now, he wondered where she was and what she was doing. He wondered what she was doing with the rest of her summer. While in Virginia Beach, she had helped him to enjoy some downtime. He hadn't realized just how hard he'd worked over the past two years. He'd almost forgotten how it felt to relax. But Dee had introduced him to activities he'd never tried. Like snorkeling. His time in Virginia Beach had been good for him. He hadn't realized just how good until he returned home and began working long hours again. It was only when he could find a few quiet moments alone that he allowed his mind to wander to thoughts of Dee, what she'd come to mean to him. He had to admit it, to himself, at least. He had fallen in love with her. What he felt for Dee was very different than what he'd felt for Amanda. And he knew, without a doubt, that Dee would never hurt him. He felt secure in his love for Dee.

As Cohen walked out to the parking garage toward his car, he was barely managing to hold his emotions in check. Dee had known about Amanda, yet she'd still taken a chance on him. She still loved him, even after overhearing him tell Tyson that he couldn't love anyone.

Instead of giving up on him, she had agreed to join him in a noncommittal, uncomplicated arrangement with only one hope--that he would finally see her for the woman she was. A woman he could trust. A woman who loved him. But he'd felt so betrayed, so manipulated, that he hadn't seen it. It had taken his talks with Dr. Frazier to finally open his eyes.

Even while overwhelmed with grief, Dr. Frazier had told Cohen that he was thankful for the time he'd had with his wife and son. At the funeral, Bob had said that having them in his life had been a blessing, even if they couldn't be with him for long. He'd said he was one of the lucky ones.

Cohen had to admit, he was lucky too. Life had knocked him down all those years ago, but he'd definitely had help getting back up. Yeah, he'd been blessed by knowing some wonderful people, starting with the professor who'd recognized what he was going through and had stepped in before he reached rock bottom. Then he'd met his best friend Tyson. And at his sister's wedding, he'd given Stacey away to a man who truly loved her, a man he was proud to call his brother. And last, but not least, there was Dee.

Dee had done something no other woman had been able to do. She had breached the wall he'd built around his heart. He loved her. He knew that now. The thought should have terrified him, and for a second it did. Then, then just as quickly, it disappeared. Because his Dee wasn't like any other woman he knew.

His Dee...

Dee was a blessing he hadn't realized he'd had. Through all his rejections, she'd continued to love him. But no more, and he couldn't blame her.

But if she gave him one last chance, he would move mountains to prove to her just how much he loved her, how much he regretted not realizing it sooner. He needed to see her. Talk to her. Beg her, if he had to. But no matter what, he refused to give her up.

Before pulling out of the parking garage, he used the app on his phone to book a flight to Memphis. Dee's brother's wedding was this weekend. He'd sent his RSVP last month, but had planned to cancel. Now, nothing would keep him away. He had to see Dee, tell her how much he loved her and throw himself on her mercy. He hoped more than anything that she would do what he hadn't been able to do in the past--forgive.

**

"Hey, you okay?"

Dee smiled over at Stacey before giving her best friend a hug. "I'm fine."

Stacey pulled back and studied Dee's features. "Are you really?"

Dee knew she couldn't lie worth a damn. "Let's just say, I'm dealing. I've kept myself busy by helping Beth with the wedding. That's helped."

"I'm glad. I was worried about you. I assume you haven't heard from Cohen."

"No, but then, I don't expect to. I really didn't expect him to show up at the wedding today, although he RSVP'd a month or so ago. But that was before things got kind of crazy, with me and his work. I guess he forgot to cancel."

She sighed. "I know I'm the last person he wants to see. He made it pretty clear there will never be anything between us. I get it this time. Immediately after Lawyer and Beth take off for their honeymoon, I'm flying out to New York for a week, compliments of Justice."

Her brother had surprised her with an early birthday present. Considering her birthday wasn't until November, the gift had warmed her heart. She knew her brothers had been very worried about her since her return from Virginia Beach. Justice had told her that she had sad eyes, and had asked her what was going on. Of course, she hadn't told him anything. She would accept the trip with the love it had been given and enjoy herself.

"Well, I hope you have fun. You deserve it."

"Thanks. I plan to take in a couple of plays and shop to my heart's content. I'm already packed. Once the wedding's over, I'm heading out for the airport."

Stacey's eyes suddenly widened. Dee was about to turn and see what her friend was staring at when Stacey grabbed her hand. "Don't look."

Dee raised a curious brow. "Why?"

"Cohen just walked in."

Dee's heart began pounding in her chest. "Cohen is here?"

"Yes. He's talking to Eli and Justice. I'm surprised he came."

Dee had to admit, so was she.

**

Cohen heard what Justice was saying, but he really wasn't listening. His attention was on the woman standing across the room talking to his sister. The woman who had his heart.

Due to flight delays, he'd barely made it to the church on time. Luckily, there was still room at the back for him to sit—the place was packed! He had seen Dee walk down the aisle as one of the bridesmaids but was pretty sure she hadn't seen him.

"You okay, Cohen?"

He glanced over at Justice. He'd always liked Dee's brothers. They were good men. And he was sure they looked after Dee the same way he'd always watched out for Stacey. So he had to wonder at Justice's question. Had the man noticed that he couldn't take his eyes off Dee? Did he wonder why? As far as Cohen knew, no one in Dee's family knew of their involvement. But maybe Dee had said something... "I'm good, thanks, Justice."

He couldn't tell the guy that he was dying to talk to his sister. It seemed getting Dee alone would be a problem. He figured there were over five hundred people at the wedding and even more at the reception. It wasn't surprising—Lawyer had a lot of friends and colleagues in Memphis. It was even rumored he might enter politics.

A short while later, Cohen watched as rice was thrown while the newly wedded couple dashed toward the waiting limo that would carry them to the airport. They would be spending a week in Barcelona before taking a cruise to Italy.

When the crowd began to disperse, he glanced around but didn't see Dee anywhere. He caught sight of his sister, though. She was standing across the room with Eli, speaking with an older couple that he remembered as

Dee's aunt and uncle from New Orleans. He quickly made his way to where she stood.

After several minutes of conversation, he turned to Stacey. "May I speak with you for a second?"

She smiled up at him. "Sure."

He led her to a private room off the huge ballroom where the wedding reception had taken place. He closed the door behind them.

"What's wrong, Cohen?"

"Where's Dee?"

"She's gone."

He frowned. "Gone where?"

Stacey frowned. "Why do you care? Don't you think you've hurt her enough?"

"I was a fool. I've made a huge mistake. I'm sorry and want her to know how I feel."

Stacey crossed her arms over her chest and narrowed her eyes. "And how *do* you feel Cohen?"

He rubbed his hand down his face in frustration. He really wanted to express his feelings to Dee before he told anyone else, but he couldn't do that without knowing where she was. He met his sister's gaze. "I love Dee, so damn much. I can't imagine my life without her, and I intend to make things up to her. Hell, I even plan to ask her to marry me. I have to have her, Stacey. She's my world."

Stacey stared at him, obviously not yet convinced. "Years ago, Cohen, you made me promise not to get involved in your love life. Remember that?"

Yes, he remembered. "That was then Stacey, this is now. You have to tell me where Dee has gone."

"If she doesn't tell you, I will."

They both glanced around to find Justice standing there, straightening his clothes. From the look at the disheveled woman standing by his side, it was apparent that Cohen and Stacey had interrupted something going on in one of the closets.

Cohen nodded. "Thanks Justice. You won't regret it.

**

Dee tossed her shopping bags on the bed. She'd been shopping all day. There was no place like New York. She couldn't help wondering what her brother was up to. A message had been left for her at the front desk that a special private dinner had been prepared for her in the Ambassador Room of the hotel. She couldn't help wondering which of Justice's romantic escapades was making it necessary that he have an alibi.

She would call him later and chew him out the way she usually did whenever he tried involving her in his shenanigans. But if he wanted to pay for her to have a special meal tonight, then she'd take advantage of it. After spending the whole day on the town, she was starving.

A short while later, she was escorted to a private room on the top floor of the building, overlooking a beautiful Manhattan at night. A table was set for two. *Two?* Did they assume she had a date? She turned to ask the maître d', only to discover the man had left, closing the door behind him.

Sighing, she moved toward the table then stopped when she sensed another presence in the room. She turned quickly and her heart began pounding in her chest. Cohen!

She stiffened. "What are you doing here?"

He came out of the shadows to stand in front of her. She didn't want to think about how good he looked. She'd heard from Stacey this morning that he'd been at the wedding. But she'd missed him, mainly because she'd immediately left for the airport.

That was yesterday. So how did he get here? More importantly, *why* was he here?

"You know why I'm here, Dee. You wished it on me. But I'm tired of having a miserable life."

Dee tried to harden her heart against anything he had to say. "You brought it on yourself."

"Yes, I did. But I'm hoping that you'll forgive me for my foolishness."

She crossed her arms over her chest. "Why should I?"

He tilted his head to that position she found irresistible, and met her gaze. "Because you love me. And someone once told me that love couldn't be turned off and on. That love didn't work that way."

If he thought he could use her words against her, then she had news for him. She lifted her chin in defiance. "And I recall you saying you didn't care how love worked. That it wasn't for you and you didn't want any part of it."

He shoved his hands in the pockets of his pants. "Yes, I did say that and I was wrong. In my defense, I honestly thought I meant it at the time. But over the last three weeks, I've discovered a few things."

"Such as?"

"Just how much I needed love in my life. And not just from anyone, but from you. I discovered that you were right. Dealing with depression doesn't make a person weak. It makes them human. But it's how someone deals with it that matters. I believed that if I ever gave my heart to someone again, I would be susceptible. But I learned something else. If I didn't make you a part of my life, I would be susceptible anyway. I guess you could say it was one of those damn-if-you-do and damn-if-you-don't situations."

She lifted a brow. "Oh, so that's what I am? A situation?"

He shook his head. "No." He took a few steps toward her, his movements mesmerizing. "What you are, Dee, is the woman I love and will always love. I think I loved you all along but refused to admit it. Why else would I have followed you to Virginia Beach if I didn't love you?"

She tried not to let his words sway her. "You rejected me, Cohen. Again."

"Yes. Because at the time I was confused."

"And now?"

"And now I'm one hundred percent certain that I want you to be a part of my life, Dee. Please say that you will."

A part of her wanted to turn around and walk away. To reject him the way he'd rejected her. But she couldn't find it in her heart to do that, because he was right. She did still love him. But hers was the forever kind of love. What kind was his?

"For how long?"

From his expression, it was obvious that her question confused him. "For how long, what?"

"For how long do you intend to love me, Cohen?"

She held her breath as he crossed the room to stand directly in front of her. He reached out, gently touching her cheek and looked deeply into her eyes. "I, Cohen Carlson, will love you, Dee Lewis, for as long as I live."

Dee couldn't stop the tears that welled in her eyes. She wanted to believe him, but when she remembered how he had rejected her, rejected her love, on three different occasions, she couldn't help but keep her guard up. "I'm afraid to put my heart on the line with you again, Cohen." Then lowering her head, she took several calming breaths. Her heart was aching so much…

She was aware of the moment he moved closer. "Dee?"

She lifted her head and gazed into his eyes. Eyes that were staring back at her with an intensity that nearly snatched the breath from her lungs. "Yes?"

"I do love you. It might have taken me a long time to admit it, but I do now. After Amanda, I thought I'd never be whole again. Then I met you." He took a deep breath. "If I have to, I will fight for you. I'll do anything to make you love me again."

"But you said…"

"And I was wrong," he countered. "I can't lose you. I love you and I need you, Dee. I intend to love you forever."

More tears formed in Dee's eyes. She couldn't stop them. Nor could she stop the softening of her heart. "And I will love you for just as long," she whispered.

He drew her into his arms and his mouth captured hers in a deep, drugging kiss that immediately began stroking her desire. When he pulled away, he said, "I love you Dee. I will keep saying it until you believe it. And I will prove it to you, every time we kiss, make love, share a meal or even just the same space. It won't matter."

He drew in a deep breath. "And you know something else I've realized?"

Dee was so filled with emotion, all she could do was shake her head.

"I realized that all this time, I've been worried about the hurt and shame I would endure if I let you into my life, knowing I couldn't give you what you need. Now I'm overwhelmed with hurt and shame because I don't have you in my life…and it's my own damn fault. Now I know what it could be like for you and me, together. And I don't want to lose my chance at a future with you."

A tender smile touched his lips. "I want you, in my bed, sharing hours of unforgettable pleasure. And I promise, I won't feel guilty about any of them."

She swiped at her tears. "That can be arranged."

I hope so." And then he was kissing her again and she forgot everything else.

When he finally broke off the kiss, he looked down at her and smiled. "Let's eat, then. We'll need our strength. After all, we have a lot of making up to do."

She nodded. Yes, they definitely did. But first, there was a question she needed him to answer for her. "How did you know where I was? I told Stacey I was coming to New York, but I didn't say what hotel I would be staying at."

He wrapped his arms around her. "Justice told me."

She arched a brow. "Justice?"

"Yes. I was trying to get Stacey to tell me where you'd gone, but she was refusing to budge, even after I confessed how much I loved you. We didn't know Justice was in the room, hiding in one of the closets."

"Why would my brother be in one of the closets?" No sooner than the question left her lips than Dee knew the answer. She quickly held up her hand. "Don't bother answering that."

Cohen nodded. "I guess he felt sorry for me, so he told me where you'd gone. I got in late last night. I had hoped to see you this morning, but the woman at the concierge desk said you left early to go shopping. So, with her help, I planned this dinner instead."

She glanced around the room. "It's so romantic. Thank you."

"I am the one who should be thanking you, for loving me and believing I deserved to be loved. And just so you know, I'm not a big fan of long-distance romances."

She smiled. "Neither am I. What do you suggest?"

"I know you love Memphis, but my job is in Florida. If I promised that we could visit Memphis regularly, would you be willing to move to Jacksonville and become my wife?"

Dee's mouth dropped open. "You want us to get married?"

He chuckled. "Yes. If I need to get down on my knees, I will, sweetheart. And I figure that while we're here in New York, we can get your engagement ring."

Dee was past trying to control the tears, at this point. "B-but don't you have to return to work?"

"I have the entire week off. They hired another neurosurgeon to help with the work load. Dr. Frazier is still on a leave of absence." Cohen got quiet for a moment. "He is a remarkable man. Even after losing everything, he isn't bitter. He is going to get some counseling, but I think he will be okay. He helped me to accept that everyone handles grief and loss in different ways."

He took her hand, pressing a kiss into her palm. "So, Dee, will you marry me?"

She couldn't contain the smile that spread across her lips. "Yes, Cohen, I will marry you. I can't remember a time when I didn't want to be your wife."

EPILOGUE

A beautiful day in June

By the powers invested in me by this great state of Tennessee, I now pronounce you husband and wife. Cohen, you may kiss your bride."

Cohen ignored the five hundred or so onlookers as he drew Dee into his arms. What mattered most to him were the minister's words that finally made Dee his wife. *His wife*. He liked the sound of that. He lowered his mouth and kissed her, and would have continued for longer than was proper, if Tyson hadn't cleared his throat. Cohen reluctantly stepped away from Dee and smiled down at her. She was simply beautiful.

Once she had accepted his marriage proposal, they'd made the decision to wait until the following June for a wedding. But Cohen had no intention of letting her leave his side, let alone live in another city. So she'd made plans to move to Jacksonville and had found a teaching job there. Closer to the wedding date, they flew to Memphis often as Dee helped her parents plan the wedding. Though she and Cohen wouldn't have minded a simple ceremony, she knew there was no sense broaching the possibility to her parents. They didn't know the meaning of the words 'small' or 'simple.'

Cohen had been surprised to discover that Dee's whole family knew of her lifelong crush on him, though she'd never mentioned it to them.

Stacey was thrilled that he'd finally come to his senses and proposed to Dee. Tyson was happy that Cohen would soon know how wonderful it was to be a married man, just as he did. Zion was ecstatic to meet Justice, the newest member of his Guarded Hearts Club.

Stacey and Eli had become parents at the beginning of the year. A green-eye son they'd named Caine had become the newest addition to the Steele family. Cohen was the proud uncle and Dee, the very happy godmother, exactly as she'd predicted. Although now, Dee was an aunt, too.

Cohen swung Dee up into his arms and carried her down the aisle as they left the church. Life was good. He was happy. There would be no more guilty pleasure on his part.

Just pleasure of the most satisfying kind.

* * *

**COMING IN THE SUMMER OF 2018,
ANOTHER BACHELOR IN DEMAND STORY,
FEATURING ZION BLACKSTONE!**

GUILTY PLEASURE

LOCKED IN TEMPTATION

By Brenda Jackson

HQN Books

Police detective Joy Ingram's commitment to protect and serve has always come first. But her connection to elite security expert Stonewall Courson is instant, undeniable, electric. And just the diversion she needs...

Enjoy a sneak peek of LOCKED IN TEMPTATION by New York Times bestselling author Brenda Jackson.

PROLOGUE

I HAVE TO keep moving.

Although her entire body ached with pain and felt as cold as ice, Mandy Clay continued to force one foot ahead of the other. Ignoring the icy wind whipping through the thin dress she wore, she continued to walk in bare feet as fast as she could, making her way someplace...anywhere but back there. That god-awful, evil place.

By now they would have discovered her missing and someone would have sounded the alarm. There was no doubt in her mind they'd be searching for her. She had no idea where she was, wasn't even sure if she was still in the United States. The only thing she knew was that she had to keep moving. It was dark and she was in some wooded area. She didn't want to think about all those sounds she was hearing. Animals? Predators? She was determined to stay alive. Sooner or later she would reach some sort of civilization. Right?

Mandy could tell it had snowed recently because the ground felt cold and squishy beneath her feet. Her toes were numb. She had to find somewhere safe. Hopefully someone would help her and call the police. Then she could tell them about the others. Those poor women...being forced to...

GUILTY PLEASURE

She slowed her pace when she thought she heard a sound. Looking through the trees, she couldn't see anything, but she could swear she heard the sound of a dog barking. Were the dogs being used to look for her? Hunt her down like the animal they'd treated her as? She wrapped her arms around herself, using all her strength to move faster. It had started snowing again. Heavier now. She felt stiff from the cold, and the pain she felt in every part of her body was almost unbearable. But she couldn't think of any of that now.

She had to keep moving. No matter what.

CHAPTER ONE

Five months later

"WHERE ARE WE GOING, Stonewall? This is not the way to my house."

Stonewall Courson brought the car to a stop at a traffic light and glanced at Joy Ingram. They had attended Striker and Margo's wedding together, and she was right. This was not the way back to her home. She was staring at him with those beautiful brown eyes that had the ability to send desire twisting in his gut and give his libido a high five whenever their gazes locked for any length of time. He would never forget the first time he'd looked into them and been totally mesmerized.

A sensual mist seemed to surround them whether they were alone or in a crowd. Those vapors were in full force now and had been from the moment he'd picked up her from her home earlier today. Stonewall had always known sexual chemistry was a powerful thing. He hadn't known just how powerful until he'd met Joy. Now he was tuned to her every breath.

Looking at her lips, he was entranced by the memory of their one and only kiss. He could recall every lip-licking detail. Just the thought sent a needy rush through his veins and made sexual excitement curl in his stomach. That single kiss was all it had taken to deeply embed her in his system. But then, he would admit the scent of her was mind-boggling, as well. In the small confines of the car, he breathed in her sensual aroma. She was wearing the same fragrance she had the night they'd met. It had been hypnotic then and it was hypnotic now.

He couldn't help but smile. It hadn't taken her long to notice he was driving in the opposite direction of where she lived. Joy was a cop, after all—a detective. Being observant and perceptive and paying attention to detail were essential parts of her job.

Today she was off the clock and she was with him. He didn't want her in cop mode. He much preferred having the element of surprise on his side. He'd known when he'd decided on this plan of action that it wouldn't be easy, given the astute person that she was. But he was determined to pull it off anyway.

"No, this is not the way to your house," he finally said. "Where we're going is a surprise." He decided to at least tell her that much.

"A surprise?"

He liked the way her brows shot up whenever she received new information. "Yes, Joy, a surprise."

He liked her name. Something about it, especially whenever he said it, made him think of pleasure, contentment and sexual bliss. They had met six months ago, at a charity function at Charlottesville's Martin Luther King Jr. Performing Arts Center. While standing in a group conversing with friends, he'd glanced around the room and seen her.

Actually, he'd caught her staring, checking him out. And she'd been pretty damn bold, not stopping when their gazes connected. He'd boldly checked her out in return, and had definitely liked what he saw. She was a beautiful woman. And the silky-looking emerald green dress she'd worn that night had complemented her body and clung to her curves. It had showcased a pair of gorgeous long legs in a pair of gold stilettos.

He'd even liked the way she'd worn her dark brown hair that night, chin-length and cut into a trendy and sassy style. But then, he would admit that he liked how she wore it now, as well. It was a lot longer and fluttered against her face while falling in fluffy waves to her shoulders. And speaking of her face…he would admit to having a thing for her high cheekbones, sable-brown complexion, straight nose and rounded chin.

On that night, even from across the room, the sexual chemistry had flared between them, nearly tripping his pulse and definitely stirring his libido in all kinds of ways. His attraction to her was stronger than any he'd ever felt, and he knew there was no way he would leave the charity ball without learning her identity. In less than twenty minutes he'd finagled an introduction. And the strange thing was, he'd always had an intense dislike for cops. At least, he had...until her.

"And since it's a surprise, that means you won't be getting any more information out of me," he added, studying her outfit. He thought the blue lace dress she was wearing today looked good on her. Sexy as hell. Clinging to her curves as if they were a lifeline. Definitely his link to sensual fantasies. He'd told her more than once today just how nice she looked.

This was only his second time seeing her in something other than a pair of dark slacks and a nondescript button-up shirt. He knew that as a police detective, she intentionally downplayed her beauty. But her looks and curves were things that couldn't be hidden no matter what she wore.

"Normally I don't like surprises."

The corners of his mouth twitched in another smile. That's what he'd heard from one reliable source, but he intended to make sure she liked this one. "Just keep an open mind, Joy. I decided it was time for our first official date."

"I thought attending Striker and Margo's wedding together was our first official date."

Turning his eyes back to the road when the traffic light turned green, he said, "Attending the wedding with me doesn't constitute a date."

"And why not?"

He quickly stole a look at her in time to see her brows shoot up again. "Because you were invited to the wedding anyway. We just happened to ride in the same car together."

She chuckled, and the feminine sound stirred something deep within him, assaulting his senses in ways he definitely wasn't used to. "I guess that's a different way to look at it, Stonewall." The way she said his name, in that sexy voice, made his insides shiver.

He knew how her mind worked. Already she was trying to figure out where they were going and what he was up to. His goal was to get her to relax and be comfortable with him. He didn't want her to think of work. All he wanted her to think about was him, just like he was thinking only of her.

On four different occasions since meeting six months ago, they'd made plans to go out on a date. However, each and every time those plans got canceled due to their work schedules. His job as a bodyguard for Summers Security Firm took him away from Charlottesville quite a lot. And hers as a police detective kept her busy solving homicides.

Whenever he was in town and their busy schedules allowed, they would meet up at a café on Monroe Street for doughnuts and coffee or grab a beer at Shady Reds Bar and Grill. However, as far as he was concerned, those brief good-to-see-you-again-and-goodbye-until-next-time encounters didn't constitute dates, either. Since meeting Joy, even though he'd never gone out with her, he hadn't been able to muster interest in any other woman. A part of him felt he wouldn't be able to move on until that changed, which was why he was taking her on a real date. A date that was long overdue.

"So, what do you have planned for this date, Stonewall?"

He chuckled. "Like I said, it's a surprise and I'm not answering any more questions, Detective, so let's talk about something else."

She didn't say anything for a minute and then, as if she'd decided to concede—for now—she said, "Margo was such a beautiful bride, wasn't she? And her wedding gown! OMG! It was simply gorgeous, and to think, she designed it herself."

Good. Stonewall figured if he kept her talking, chances were she wouldn't think about where they were going. Hopefully she would let her guard down and relax. Joy had met Margo while working a case that had her racing against time trying to solve a deadly puzzle that had placed Margo's life in danger.

"Yes, Margo looked beautiful and her gown was gorgeous," he agreed. "Striker is a lucky man. Margo's a lucky woman. I'm glad they have each other."

Stonewall truly meant it, although he still found it hard to believe that Striker Jennings, one of his two best friends, had gotten married that day. Like him, Striker had enjoyed his life as a single man too much to think about getting serious with any one woman. Until Striker was assigned as a bodyguard to protect Margo Connelly. The man Stonewall figured would never fall in love had done that very thing.

The same held true for his other best friend, Quasar Patterson, who was engaged to marry a woman by the name of Randi Fuller. After both his friends married, that would leave him as the lone bachelor with all the women. However, Joy was the only woman he thought about. Constantly.

"I thought it was pretty neat how both of Margo's uncles walked her down the aisle."

"I thought so, too," Stonewall agreed. "Margo's quick acceptance of Roland into her life is special."

Roland Summers. CEO of Summers Security Firm and his boss as well as a man he considered a good friend. Years ago, Roland had been a cop for the Charlottesville Police Department when he'd discovered some of his fellow officers on the take. Before he could blow the whistle, he'd been framed for murder and sentenced to prison for fifteen years. Roland's wife, Becca, had refused to accept Roland's fate and worked hard to get him a new trial. In retaliation, the dirty cops had killed not only Becca but also Roland's half brother and sister-in-law—Margo's parents.

"Roland looks good. It's hard to believe that only six months ago he was in the hospital, fighting for his life."

Roland had been shot earlier that year in an attempted carjacking. Just so happened, it was the same night that Stonewall and Joy had met.

"And it was good seeing Randi again," Joy said.

Randi was a psychic investigator. She and Joy had met earlier this year when the two worked together to solve the very case involving Margo. Several people lost their lives before the assassin had been taken down. Stonewall had never believed in psychic powers until meeting Randi. Her help on the case had been instrumental and had made a believer out of him.

"I wouldn't be here today if it wasn't for Randi," Joy continued. "I will never forget the day she saved my life."

Stonewall nodded. From what he'd heard, Joy had been about to drink a cup of coffee tainted with poison. Luckily, thanks to her psychic powers, Randi had detected it and stopped Joy just seconds before it was too late.

"Randi and Quasar look good together," Joy added. "And just the thought that they're engaged is wonderful."

Stonewall smiled in agreement, happy that for the time being, Joy was so caught up in the wedding and the people she'd seen that day that she'd temporarily forgotten she had no idea where they were going.

"And Carson Granger looks simply radiant pregnant," he heard Joy add. "So do Caden Granger's wife, Shiloh, and Dalton's wife, Jules. I can't believe there are three pregnant women in the same family and all due around the same time. How cool is that? Sheppard Granger will definitely have his hands full becoming a father and grandfather."

Stonewall couldn't help chuckling. Shep's wife, Carson, would be having a baby in a few weeks, around the same time that two of his sons' wives would be having theirs. "Yes, Shep will definitely have his hands full. But if anyone can handle an expanded family with ease, it would be Shep," he said of the man he considered a father figure and mentor.

Dalton, Shep's youngest son, was almost twenty-nine. That meant Shep would be starting all over with the diapers, preschool, high school, college…practically everything. Like Roland, Shep had been locked up for fifteen years for a crime he didn't commit, and if starting over in fatherhood was what he wanted, then Stonewall was happy for him.

When Joy ran out of people to discuss from the wedding, he kept the conversation going by telling her about his recent trips to Dubai, Australia, Thailand and Cape Town. His extensive travels were part of his job assignment to protect wealthy businessman Dakota Navarro, who preferred to be called Dak. Over the past six months, his and Dak's relationship had moved beyond that of client and bodyguard to good friends.

Stonewall brought the car to a stop. "Well, here we are."

He watched as Joy looked out the window before glancing back at him. "A private jet?"

He smiled. "Yes, and no, it's not mine. It's belongs to Dakota Navarro. He loaned it to me."

She lifted a brow. "Loaned it to you."

"Yes, he loaned me the plane and the pilot."

"Why?"

Stonewall unsnapped his seat belt and smiled at her. "Because he's aware of how I've been looking forward to finally taking you out on a real date. Dak's also aware that jet-setting around the world protecting him is one of the reasons I couldn't do so. He figured the least he could do was help our romance along."

"Our romance?"

"Yes." There was no need to tell her that romance hadn't been the word Dak used. The international playboy and businessman considered each date with a woman as a conquest of the most sexual kind.

"And just where is this jet supposed to be taking us?"

"Martha's Vineyard. I've made reservations for dinner." Anticipating her next question, he added, "And I promise to have you home before midnight."

What's next in store for Joy and Stonewall?
Find out when LOCKED IN TEMPTATION
by New York Times bestselling author Brenda Jackson,
goes on sale in August 2017.

GUILTY PLEASURE

Pre-Order it now!

Amazon –

https://www.amazon.com/Locked-Temptation-Protectors-Brenda-Jackson-ebook/dp/B01N2G63MZ/ref=sr_1_1?s=books&ie=UTF8&qid=1495476168&sr=1-1&keywords=locked+in+temptation+by+brenda+jackson

Barnes and Noble -
http://www.barnesandnoble.com/w/locked-in-temptation-brenda-jackson/1124690538?ean=9781460399965

Google Play-
https://play.google.com/store/books/details/Brenda_Jackson_Locked_in_Temptation?id=jGt9DQAAQBAJ&hl=en

Kobo – https://www.kobo.com/us/en/ebook/locked-in-temptation

WELCOME TO THE EXCITING READING WORLD OF
NEW YORK TIMES AND USA TODAY BEST SELLING AUTHOR BRENDA JACKSON

Get Your Free Brenda Jackson App

Available for iPhone, iPad and Android. Scan the QR Code with your smartphone, or search Brenda Jackson in your app store!

Want to receive Brenda Jackson's monthly newsletter? Click here!

http://www.brendajackson.net/?page_id=57

Visit Brenda's website at –

www.brendajackson.net

BRENDA JACKSON BOOKS

There are over 10 million Brenda Jackson books in print.

Click here for a printable book list of all Brenda Jackson books, the breakdown of the books in their respective series and the order of books.

http://www.brendajackson.net/?page_id=10

Visit my website at – www.brendajackson.net

Download my FREE Brenda Jackson APP on your smart phone!

BRENDA JACKSON

MEET THE GRANGERS AND THE PROTECTORS

COMING IN DECEMBER 2017

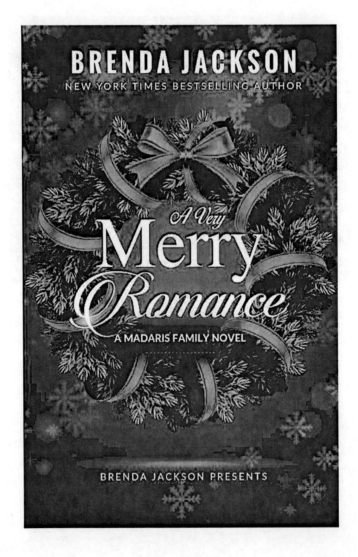

ABOUT THE AUTHOR

BRENDA JACKSON is a die "heart" romantic who married her childhood sweetheart Gerald forty-four-years ago and still proudly wears the "going steady" ring he gave her when she was fifteen. Their marriage produced two sons, Gerald Jr and Brandon, of whom Brenda is extremely proud. Because she's always believed in the power of love, Brenda's stories have happy endings and credits Gerald for being her inspiration.

A New York Times and USA Today Bestselling author of over one- hundred romance titles, Brenda divides her time between, family, writing and traveling. You may write Brenda at P.O Box 28267, Jacksonville, Florida 32226; her e-mail address at authorbrendajackson@gmail.com and her website at www.brendajackson.net

Download the FREE Brenda Jackson app on your smartphone and "Like" her Face Book Readers' Page at - Facebook.com/BrendaJacksonAuthor

* Photo Credit - Pete Stenberg Photography

CPSIA information can be obtained
at www.ICGtesting.com
Printed in the USA
LVOW10s1527271017
554035LV00009B/540/P